# LEGACIES

*Sharon Kay*

Writer's Showcase

San Jose  New York  Lincoln  Shanghai

# Legacies

Writer's Showcase
an imprint of iUniverse, Inc.

For information address:
iUniverse, Inc.
5220 S. 16th St., Suite 200
Lincoln, NE 68512
www.iuniverse.com

Any resemblance to actual people and events is purely coincidental. This is a work of fiction.

ISBN: 0-595-23981-1

Printed in the United States of America

*In loving memory of my sister, Wonda Joy, who never had the chance to experience the dance of life.*

# Acknowledgements

I wish to acknowledge the people who stood behind me and made this possible. To my husband, J.T....your belief in me has been incredible. Thank you for all the dinners, you've cooked so that I could do my "work". I love you tremendously. To my children, Shannon and Kristi and their spouses Candi and Todd...I wish this somehow gives you a measure of pride, thank you for your years of encouragement and insistence that I do something with this story. You are the pride of my life. To my grandchildren, who hold the keys to my heart, Erin, Trevor, John-Michael, Hannah, Corianne, Peyton and Noah...I leave this my legacy to you.

# CHAPTER 1

❀

"*R*yan!"

The name came tearing out of Joy's throat as she bolted upright in bed. Thunder screamed its blood-curdling call through the night while lightning streaked across the darkened sky causing it to take on the appearance of dawn.

This was not the first time a storm snatched her from the wonderful place deep in her dreams where she and Ryan could be together. Still shaky from being yanked out of her dream by the storm she dropped back against the headboard of her bed and lifted shaking hands up to her face. It was wet. As always when she dreamed of Ryan she cried, even in her deepest sleep. She pushed her thick chestnut hair away from her eyes letting her fingers touch and linger briefly in the slightly raised scar that ran down the right side of her face. The scar was a constant reminder of that stormy night so long ago.

"Ryan," she repeated, this time in a broken whisper as she pulled the cool, unused pillow next to hers and hugged it tightly. Each time he was ripped from her dreams the pain residing deep inside her increased. Seven years had passed leaving Joy with deep agonizing dreams and a terror of storms. She called out to the darkness seeking answers to the questions raging in her mind. When would the memories of that night fade and when would she be able to appreciate summer storms again. No one was there in the darkened house to give them to her. No one was there to comfort her except Patches, her calico cat, which chose that moment to leap onto the bed. She gave a languid stretch and began rubbing affectionately against Joy's leg. Mewing softly, it seemed she was trying to tell her, it's all right, I'm here. You're not alone.

Pulling the cat into her arms and hugging her tightly against her chest Joy whispered to the cat as though in answer, "that's right, huh Patches, my love. I have you. I know there is nothing to be afraid of. I'm just a big silly girl allowing storms to remind me of too damn much." Caressing the warm furry creature, Joy drifted back to the past allowing memories of long ago to flood her thoughts. Storms had a way of bringing her back in time to the night she married Ryan Young. It appeared to her that with all the beautiful things to remember about that night, the storm was always the first memory to surface. Thunder and lightning. Lots of it.

She stifled a scream as another clap of thunder sounded, this time strong enough to rattle the windowpanes. Lightning momentarily brightened the room giving an impression of a light switch being quickly turned on and off. The pouring rain beat a tune of its own as it fell from the eaves and collected into puddles beneath the window and the fragrance of rain-soaked soil floated in through the slightly raised window of Joy's bedroom. Squeezing her eyes tightly shut and covering her ears with her hands, Joy tried to shut out the sights and sounds of the storm. "Stop! Stop! Please stop!" she chanted while rocking back and forth on the edge of her bed. Suspended some-where between nightmare and wakefulness she became lost in the jumble of thoughts where past and present fused together with only the raging storm and her cat to keep her company. Eventually her mind registered another sound in the house, a shrill insistent ring-ing. Caught in the web of her painful memories, Joy absentmindedly reached for her alarm clock. She pressed the snooze button but the ringing continued. Try as she might, she couldn't identify the sound. Forcing her eyes open she shook her head to clear the fog that had taken up residence there for the last few minutes. Awareness set in and she realized the sound she heard was coming from the telephone. She forced her eyes to focus on the bedside alarm clock. It was two a.m. Tears were still streaming down her face and she looked like a lost child, one who had just realized that they are actually separated from their loved ones. The look was born of torment. The look before panic sets in. If one ever paid close attention while looking into Joy's eyes, they would see perpetual panic lurking just beneath the great softness that so directly looked back.

Wondering who could be calling her at this time of night, she stumbled through the darkened hallway groping her way to the kitchen to answer the phone and stop its incessant ringing. Lost as she was, she'd totally forgotten the recently installed telephone in her bedroom. "Hello," her voice was soft and a little breathy as a result of the turmoil her mind was in.

"Hello, may I speak to Joy Young, please?" The caller on the other end responded with a crisp voice.

"This is she," she replied to the cool but vaguely familiar voice on the other end of the phone. Her heart began a sporadic rhythm in response to the caller's voice speaking to her at this godless hour. She knew this voice, but couldn't place it. It was a good voice, one that immediately summoned good feelings in her. A voice from her past, but from where? God but she hated when her mind left on vacation without her.

"Joy, this is Hank. Hank Morgan?" His voice was deep, rich and somewhat melodic and took on a questioning tone when stating his full name.

Joy's heart leapt at mention of his name and began a rhythm of its own, two-stepping in her chest. She was so surprised by the call that she stood there absolutely at a loss for words.

Taking her speechlessness as hesitation Hank continued, thinking perhaps she'd forgotten him as well. "You know, Hank from New Orleans. Do you remember who I am Joy or have you forgotten me as well?"

"Hank!" It was only one word but that was all she could get out and even it came across as a squeak. He'd caught her off guard. She cleared her throat and tried again. "Hank, is it really you? Goodness, it's been a lifetime since I've heard your voice." Her voice grew stronger and more energized as reality sank in. Hank Morgan. She was talking to Hank, one third of the "trio" as they were known in high school. "Thank God you're still alive. I thought you hadn't made it back from the Army. When did you get out? Why haven't you called before? Where are you?" Forgetting the raging storm outside and the fact that this call was practically in the middle of the night, Joy could only think of this moment and that Hank was on the other end of the phone line. She bombarded him with questions.

Her questions were like sleet to Hank, indeed Joy herself was like sleet to him, beautiful to see and hear but sharp, stinging and dangerous to be around. This call was harder than he expected. He had not called her to make small talk and it was taking all of his resolve to remain firm and not let her voice get to him like it did so many years ago and still did in his dreams. Evading her questions Hank condescendingly responded, "I did not call to make small talk. A-hem," he cleared his throat, and continued. "This is not a social call and I want you to know that I'm making this call against my better judgment, however, Charles requested I do this, so, I'm doing it." Before she could respond he hurried on, "Charles, as I said before, asked me to call you. He's in the hospital and needs to see you. It's his request that you come back home immediately because he hasn't much time."

Questions and thoughts chased around in Joy's head. Her father-in-law was in the hospital and asking for her. He wanted her to go home, go back to New Orleans. Oh, the word home sounded so good, especially hearing Hank say it. But home held so many memories. Bittersweet memories of her life and love of long ago.

Hank continued, "And Joy, since I made the phone call I just as soon add my two cents," he hesitated.

Joy took advantage of his hesitation, "and what might your two cents be?"

His words were sharp, "don't let him down as well."

His last words astounded her. It felt as though he'd reached through the phone lines and physically slapped her face. Why was he being so mean to her? The question flooded her mind and caused a long forgotten reaction to surface. He'd hurt her feelings flinging her back into her childhood where she'd experienced many times the same feeling his words summoned in her. Her chest caught fire and the heat seared her from her chest upwards ending in her blazing face. Tears smarted her eyes as she swallowed hard and tried to speak. "Hank, why are you being so cold? Don't you remember everything we once shared? I don't remember doing anything to hurt you, but you seem intent on acting like a stranger to me. I know it's been a long time, but we were so close, the three of us, you, Ryan and me. I thought nothing could ever come between the trio." Sounding dejected she added with a sigh, "I guess I was wrong." Her voice caught on a sob as she ended her tirade.

Her voice was working its magic on Hank. On the other end of the line Hank felt his resolve to be hard on her being washed away by her words until he heard her speak Ryan's name. How dare she bring his name up, after everything that had happened? Hearing his best friend's name come from Joy's lips helped snap him back to reality. Pulling back his cool reserve and hugging it tightly around himself like a cloak shielding his heart, he ignored her remarks asking her instead if she intended on honoring Charles's request.

Trying hard to match her voice tone with his Joy couldn't help herself and asked one more question, "Will you be there to meet me? The idea of returning to New Orleans unnerves me a bit."

His response was cold, as a matter of fact it was like dry ice compared to his conversation a few minutes earlier and each word stung Joy to her core. "No Joy, I won't be there for you. You see, someone else needs me more than you do and I don't let people I love down. Go to St. Charles General Hospital and ask for Dr. Peters. He is Charles's doctor and good friend. He'll take care of you." He heard a quiet sob escape from Joy as she listened to him. One part of him wanted to be able to offer her come degree on comfort but the other part wanted to hurt her the way she had hurt him and probably everyone that ever loved her. He steeled himself against the sound of her soft sobbing and couldn't resist one last stab, hoping he could erase some of his pain by giving it to her. "As for your return causing you some discomfort, I'm afraid that is something you have to deal with. Maybe you'll think twice before running away again when so many need you."

Tears streamed down Joy's cheeks as she heard the distinct click of the connection being broken. She stood there holding the phone in her hand, staring at it like it was the strangest thing she'd ever seen. How dare he talk to her like that! It was clear that Hank didn't know what he was talking about, saying that she'd run away when so many needed her. The truth of it was that the only person who ever needed her was Ryan and he was gone. Her in-laws didn't need her, they were the ones that sent her away and Hank had been in the Army when she'd left New Orleans. Well, she couldn't worry about all Hank's nonsense now. She would talk to him in New Orleans and straighten him out on a few things, you could bet your booty on that, she resolved as she finally replaced the receiver in its cradle. Just her return to the city that had given her so much just to take it away again was worry enough. Grabbing a tissue Joy wiped the tears from her face and thought about the injustice of it all. Her philosophy was that life was a series of circles whereby you'd finish one circle and go on to complete a new and larger circle, growing and changing as you went along, except that she felt she was caught in some sort of warp zone, whereby she could catch a glimpse of the next circle but just as she stepped over, gravity would go haywire and throw her back causing her to repeat the same circle, never allowing her to move on to the next one. Today was no exception and once again Joy's philosophy was proven true. The familiar nightmare was turning into reality and as usual Joy felt like she was left alone to face the demons in this the worst circle of her life. Hank's call snatched her from the safe cocoon she'd woven for herself and was throwing her back into the turmoil of the past. Come home, come home, come home. The words repeated themselves in Joy's head sounding like a funeral dirge laying a burden on her heart with each repetition. It wasn't just the thought of returning to New Orleans that troubled Joy; it was the idea that her life was about to change again. She knew this to be true, call it woman's intuition or whatever you want to, but it was going to change. The change would affect other people beside herself. The desire to return to New Orleans was always with Joy, but the fear of change and the painful memories the city held for her were like a wall keeping her away.

A lot had happened in the last seven years. Building the wall that held her away from the home and people she loved most in the world wasn't the only thing Joy had done. She had also gotten engaged. Her fiancé was Shaze Martin. It was Shaze she thought of now as she began making plans for returning to New Orleans. How would he take the news of her leaving town? Every time she tried talking to him about New Orleans he'd grow furious. Now she had to tell him she was returning there. Almost like an omen indicating Shaze's possible reaction, a loud boom of thunder sounded. Awareness of the storm brought her back to where she'd started. She looked at the clock on the coffeemaker as she turned the switch on. It read two-thirty. She felt like she'd lived an entire lifetime in the thirty minutes since being abruptly awakened. She sat there alone in her neat little kitchen wondering what she should do next. The thought of calling Beth, her employee and best friend or Shaze at this hour was not a pleasant one. She sat down waiting for the coffee to brew and went over the conversation with Hank, pushing to the rear her excitement at the idea of his calling her and concentrating instead on the purpose of his call. He'd said only that Charles was in the hospital. They never got around to the nature of his illness. Damn, how stupid could she get? She'd been so wrapped up in hearing Hank's voice that she'd completely forgotten to ask what was wrong with Charles. Thinking hard, she remembered the doctor's name. Hank had told her she was to go to St. Charles General and ask for a Dr. Peters. With trembling fingers she picked the receiver up and dialed information. Before she could stop herself she was calling the hospital and asking for the doctor.

Surprisingly he was there and answered the page. His voice was deep and kind and he told Joy Charles had suffered a severe heart attack. As the doctor's words sank in, her head cleared and the only concern she had at the moment was for Charles. Her voice trembled with disbelief as she questioned the doctor.

"Charles has had a heart attack? Oh God! I can't believe this." Joy hauled a chair to the kitchen phone and plopped down in it. "How did it happen? When?"

"Ms Young, I'm afraid I don't have much to tell you. I can tell you that I know how very much he wants you here."

"But, Dr. Peters it's been so long since I've been involved with this family. I haven't spoken to Charles or Mamie in at least five years. Why is he asking for me after all this time?" Her confusion at Charles' request manifested itself in the faltering tone of her voice.

"Ms Young, I know this is hard for you. It probably brings up things you had laid to rest, but I really think you should come to New Orleans as soon as possible. Tonight if you could arrange it. I think Charles would rest better if I could tell him you were on your way. Perhaps I could..."

Joy could hear the doctor's southern drawl but was lost again in her thoughts. Her mind took off on a tangent of its own at the thought of returning to New Orleans. What would it be like to go back? Back to that hospital? It had been seven long years, but was it long enough to have eased the pain?

"Ms Young, are you still there? Uh…hello, Ms Young…"

Realizing she had slipped back into her memories, Joy snapped back to the present, "Oh, Dr. Peters, I'm very sorry. Yes, yes of course you can tell Charles I'm coming." Pausing for a brief moment, Joy added, "and Dr. Peters, you're right, it will be hard to come back to New Orleans. I knew the time would come when I'd have to face the past. I just hadn't planned on it happening like this." Her voice held traces of uncertainty as she spoke of returning to face the past. It would indeed be a rough time for her, rougher than anyone could imagine. In a voice that suddenly sounded stronger and more determined, Joy stated, "I'll be on the next available flight and I'll come straight to St. Charles General."

"Great. I'll tell Charles you're on your way." Doctor Peters let out a sigh of relief as he heard Joy say she'd come to New Orleans, although his fear of her refusing had been unfounded. From what he could remember and from the things Charles had told him she had always been a shy, sweet girl who'd always considered other people's needs before her own, always putting aside her feelings to help when she was needed and it seemed that she hadn't changed. But she had changed, she was no longer a girl, the doctor reminded himself. She was a woman now. A young woman who has had to bear more than her share of problems, but still the kind loving person the Youngs had all fallen in love with.

"Dr. Peters?"

"Yes?"

"Thank you. Thanks for caring and for being there for Charles."

The doctor's voice grew soft as emotion swelled in him. "There is no need to thank me as I should thank you instead. Charles has been my friend for a long time and he's confided in me concerning many personal things in his life, you among them. Charles will be so happy that you're coming back and I feel safe in saying that I don't think you'll regret coming back to New Orleans. But, Ms Young…"

"Yes?"

"I'd advise you to be strong. Things may not be what they seem."

Puzzled by his words, Joy asked, "What do you mean?"

Thinking it best to let her find out what his words meant, the doctor answered instead, "I've got to go now. Goodbye and again, thank you."

Would this night ever give her answers instead of more questions, she wondered. A frown creased her near perfect forehead as speculations of the meaning of the doctor's words manifested themselves in her mind. Concluding that she had no time to fret about what might be in store for her, she dispelled her ambivalence, poured herself a cup of coffee and began to make plans for her unexpected trip. Deciding to leave the store in Beth's care, she dialed her valued employee and best friend's number. Waiting for Beth to answer, Joy dropped her weary body in a chair. Her legs were trembling and her knees felt weak. She felt nauseous as she thought again of her impending trip. It had been such a long time since she'd left and gone to Los Angeles to open the jewelry store. Her jewelry store now. It had been a wedding present to Ryan and her from Ryan's parents. They'd had such high hopes and big dreams for the store. For their future. Dreams that had never come to pass. Dreams. Wonderful dreams turned into nightmares. Storms. Loud noises. Flashes of light. Death. And now, to go back to where it all happened…Oh God, she prayed as fear reared its ugly head, please help me get through this.

Beth's disgruntled bark on the other end of the phone brought Joy back to the present. "Hello…hello…hey, if you're on the line and want to talk to me, speak up. You don't want to talk, then go to hell…" Her bluntness indicated her displeasure at being awakened in the middle of the night by what she presumed to be a prank caller.

"Oh, Beth…wait, don't hang up. It's me, Joy."

"Joy? What's wrong? What time is it?" Beth Segal sat up in bed instantly alert as trepidation replaced the irritation caused by the late night call.

"It's a little after three a.m. Beth. I'm sorry to call you at this time of the morning. I need your help." Cutting off the tide of questions she knew would be forthcoming from Beth, she quickly continued. "I really don't have time to explain everything to you right now. I need you to run the store and to take care of my house and Patches for me. I have to go to New Orleans tonight and I don't know how long I'll be gone, but it shouldn't be more that a few days."

Joy's attempt at deterring Beth's inquisitiveness failed as Beth began to pump her for more information. "A few days? Why New Orleans? When are you leaving? Running away from your responsibilities huh?" Beth said the last jokingly, referring to the fact that the annual inventory was to begin in a couple of days.

Joy cringed. Responsibilities? Running from responsibilities? Something inside her wanted to scream shrilly at Beth's accusation, but her voice was soft and wistful as she replied, "Beth, if it were only that simple." Then even more softly, almost inaudibly, Joy replied, "all my responsibilities in New Orleans ended a long time ago." In a stronger voice, Joy repeated the reason for her call. "Look, can you stay at my house for a few days and help me out by looking after things? You can do it all as well as I can."

"Sure girl. You know I'll do whatever you need me to do. Just tell me when." Beth, knowing Joy's request was one born of urgency, put aside all kidding. Joy wasn't the type of person to shirk responsibilities and Beth was genuinely happy to help her out.

"Good. Move in tomorrow. I'm leaving for New Orleans tonight. I'll call you when I get there. Okay?"

"Wait! Joy. Don't hang up yet. Damn girl, you are in a hurry aren't you?" Without giving Joy a chance to answer, Beth asked hesitantly, "what about Shaze? I don't mind running the store, but what will he say about that? You know how asinine he can be…"

Joy cut in with her reply; "Shaze shouldn't be a problem for you because I'm asking him to come with me."

"Huh! I hope he goes with you, but he'll probably make up some excuse not to go," Beth's words dripped with sarcasm.

"Come on Beth, lighten up. I can't take this from you right now. I don't have the time and I'm not in the mood for it. I'm sure if Shaze can't come with me, his excuse will be legitimate." Joy's voice barely masked the exhaustion she felt, because of the hostility between her friend and Shaze. "You two really need to work out this animosity between you, because truthfully, I'm fed up with the mistrust you have of each other and it's getting on my nerves." Joy definitely was not in the mood for this discussion and hoped Beth detected as much in her tone.

"Hey, keep your drawers on," Beth said defensively. "I'd settle this with him anytime I could corner him and you know it. But, you're right, this is not the time and you do sound as if you need support right now and not my bitching. Don't worry, girl, I'll take good care of the store and of my friend Patches. You just take care of yourself and your business," and as an afterthought she added, "and be careful. Okay?"

"Thank you Friend. I owe you one."

Yeah, a big one, Beth thought as she told Joy goodbye and hung up the phone. She wondered if Joy would succeed in getting Shaze to go with her. Well, if he does go, she mused, at least he'll be out my hair, and good riddance. Shaze Martin was bad news, at least as far as Beth was concerned. She'd sensed it the minute she first laid eyes on him. There was something about the look in his eyes when he thought no one was watching that made her uneasy. He never looked anyone straight in the eyes when speaking to them. He just gave her the creeps and that was all there was to it.

Joy hung up the phone and was startled to hear it ring immediately. Thinking it was Beth again, she was surprised to hear Shaze's voice.

"Hello, Sweetheart. Hope I didn't wake you. The thunder awakened me and I thought of you." His voice was thick with sleepiness, enhancing his already sexy voice. "I thought I'd call and see how you're holding up in this storm. Are you all right?"

Touched by his concern, Joy felt her heart swell with affection. "Shaze, you know me so well. Thank you for checking on me. In fact, I was about to call you."

"Call me? At this time? Because of the storm?" He knew the effect storms had on Joy and was ready to comfort her if she needed him. "Do you need me to come…"

"Whoa, hold on. One question at a time, okay? I was about to call you because," she took a deep breath, "I need your help."

"What's wrong Joy? Are you in some sort of trouble?" Fully awake now, Shaze turned his full attention to what she was saying. He knew Joy wasn't prone to seeking help from anyone and her sudden admittance to needing help intrigued him.

"No, Sweetheart, at least I don't think I'm in any trouble." Detecting the concern in his voice and knowing how easy it was to upset him, especially if he thought she was in any sort of danger, she replied, "I have to leave right away."

"Leave? Where do you have to go?"

"To New Orleans."

"Why New Orleans?" his voice grew pensive.

Shakily, Joy told him of her long distance phone call. "It seems Charles, my father-in-law, was just admitted to the hospital and is asking for me. I promised I'd be on my way ASAP."

"Why is he asking for you? I thought you weren't in touch with him anymore." Shaze's voice suddenly chilled.

In response to his apparent rigidity, Joy's voice hardened, her exasperation sounding clearly, "I don't know why he's wanting me. It seems he's had a heart attack. He wants me there and that's all I know." Concern for Charles overtook her and her voice trembled as she tried to soften Shaze's resolve. "Shaze, the doctor is really worried about Charles's condition. He feels that Charles will rest better once he's seen me."

"Great, run back to New Orleans," his voice was full of sarcasm. "I don't understand why you feel you need to do anything for anyone over there. You don't owe them anything. All New Orleans holds for you is sorrow and bad memories, remember?" His tone was brisk and Joy knew he wasn't happy with her decision to respond to Charles's request.

"Yes, I remember," she whispered softly, and then letting out a sigh, she pursued the issue. "Please, Shaze, don't make this any harder than it already is. As I said earlier, I need your help. Are you still willing to help me?"

Petulantly, he replied, "depends on what kind of help you're wanting. What can I do for you?" Gone was the soft tender concern that had filled his voice just a few minutes ago. His voice now sounded chilled and brittle.

"You could come with me," she said in a voice on the verge of breaking, burdened by the anxiety of the trip and Shaze's unconcealed displeasure.

"Come with you?" he echoed her question with one of his own. "I suppose I could go with you, but what about the store? Wouldn't it be better if I stayed and looked after it while you're gone?"

His procrastination in giving her an answer to her question caused her some apprehension. Why didn't he want to go to New Orleans? Was he running from something? Pushing these thoughts behind her she replied rather forcefully, "Everything is already taken care of. Beth will see to the store, my house, and my cat. I need your support on this trip Shaze. Will I have it?" Joy, pumped with adrenaline and anxious to resolve this and get on with her plans, became irritated.

"Okay, okay, calm down. I'll come with you. What time are you leaving?" He still sounded reluctant.

"I don't know. I can't think straight. I don't even know if any flights are going out, with this storm blowing. The calls and the storm, God it's almost too much."

Picking up on her agitation and concluding that perhaps a trip to New Orleans wasn't a bad idea after all, he changed his tune, "don't worry, Love. I'll take care of booking the flight. You just take care of your packing. I'll be over as soon as I throw a few things together."

Grateful for his change of heart, Joy let out a sigh of relief. "Thank you Shaze. That would be a great help. Just the thought of returning to New Orleans alone and with this storm…" she shuddered.

"Don't think about it, just concentrate on your packing. And Joy?"

"Yes?" Now what? Her weary mind asked as she heard the soft response on the other end of the phone.

"I love you."

Numbly and without answering she hung up the phone. She whispered into the stormy night, "I'm going home," and walked out of the room to get ready for the trip.

# CHAPTER 2

*F*illed with mixed emotions Joy boarded the plane two hours after the call from New Orleans. Although grateful their timing was right in being able to secure seats on this flight she was distraught at being so lucky. Trepidation for what lay ahead was settling in her stomach leaving her with a sensation of having eaten a ton of steel. She was afraid. She had no fear of flying, her fear rested in the storm and what waited for her in New Orleans.

Shaze patted her hand as the pilot's announcement came over the speaker welcoming them and asking them to remain belted in their seats until further notice, as it looked like they might be in for a bumpy ride.

Par for the course, Joy thought, regarding storms as bad omens.

Stealing a glance at Joy, Shaze noticed small beads of perspiration on her face. Her chocolate colored eyes loomed large in her slender face giving her the appearance of a frightened doe. She had haphazardly piled the mass of deep brown curls on top of her head imprisoning the unruly tendrils in a beautiful gold and jade comb. Escaping the confines of the comb a few renegade curls touched her face here and there, some of them gently sticking where perspiration had popped out. Beads of perspiration lined her full upper lip and Shaze had to hold back a surge of desire to kiss the inviting lips. He reached over instead, and gently wiped the beads away. Smiling, he reached down and took her hand into his. It was cold and clammy, attesting to her nervousness. Hoping to distract her attention from the storm, he asked her how she was truly feeling about returning to New Orleans.

"I love New Orleans, Shaze. I planned on returning—someday when I would be ready to face the memories that wait for me there. I just never in my life, expected to be going back on these conditions. To have Charles ask for me—," Joy shook her head in disbelief.

"When was the last time you heard from Charles, Joy?" Shaze could see the expression in her eyes change from fright to sadness as the memories began to stir and come to life.

"He kept in touch with me for a couple of years after my move to Los Angeles. You know, he'd call in and ask me if I needed any help with the store and things like that. Just talking to him reminded me so much of my life with Ryan and I suspect he realized that, because his calls became fewer and further between, then they just stopped altogether." Joy looked at her hands and fingered the engagement ring on her left hand. Her action was not lost on Shaze.

Rubbing the ring with his finger he looked at Joy, "you know, Babe, we're engaged and I know you were once married, but other than that—I know very little about you. How about you filling me in on the old past, huh?" Shaze squeezed Joy's hand and nodded in acquiescence when she looked at him with dubious eyes.

"I don't know, Shaze. I don't know if I'm ready."

"Don't be frightened, Joy. It's the past. Remember that. Nothing you tell me can actually hurt you again. Maybe it's time you exorcise the memories that still throw you for a loop. Look, I've read a lot of self-improvement books and they all say the same thing. Talk about what's haunting you. If you get it out in the open, it will become less painful." And as an afterthought, he added, "after all, if you can't tell me, then who can you tell?"

"Maybe you're right. But it's a long story, Shaze. My life has been far from typical." Joy tried unsuccessfully to make light of her words.

Spreading out his arms in a sweeping gesture, he answered, "we have practically a cross country flight ahead of us, Honey, talk to me. Okay?" He squeezed her hand again, in encouragement.

Taking a deep breath, she began her story. Born in Lafayette, the center of Cajun Country, she was an only child. She told him of Bubba, her closest friend and of the good times they shared. These were good memories. She told him of the afternoon that began the end of her life, as she'd known it. While sharing with Shaze the details, Joy closed her eyes and let the words play in her mind, like watching a movie. "Bubba, what do you wanna be when you grow up?" Joy and her next-door neighbor were lying in a field of clover looking up at the great blue dome of the sky, imagining various shapes out of the billowing clouds.

"Look see that pirate's ship," Bubba sat up pointing to the sky and totally ignoring Joy's question.

"Forget your stupid pirate's ship Bubba and quit ignoring my question. You always do that and it makes me mad." Joy sat up and removed the clover stem that she had been chewing on. "I guess if you don't want to talk about grown-up things, I'll just get my craw-fishing pole and go home." She moved toward the gully bank where their fishing poles were stuck in holes offering support leaving their hands free for pointing.

Bubba jumped up, "Ah, Joy, c'mon don't go. I'll answer your stupid question."

Joy shot the ten-year-old boy a look that made him change his tune.

"Ah, maybe on second thought your question wasn't that stupid. I guess when I grow up I want to be rich. No matter what I do, I just want to be rich. And I want to fly planes. You know, those jets that pass over and leave that white streak in the sky. One day I'm gonna make that streak. What do you wanna be Joy?"

A dreamy look came over Joy's little white face. "I want to be a wife and a mother and I want to move away but not too far and my husband is gonna love me and tell me I'm beautiful and we're gonna do fun things with our children."

To a ten-year-old boy Joy's answer was rotten. "Joy you're no fun. Your answer is stupid. Don't you want to do something exciting, like fly a plane or discover something like a treasure?"

Joy shook her head as she looked at her friend who shared the same birthday as hers, feeling years older than their shared ten years. "Bubba, life holds enough excitement without having to go out and look for it. You go ahead and learn how to fly your planes and I'll look for my husband. Then one day, my husband and I will fly on your plane to someplace you think is exciting. How's that?"

Bubba's answer was drowned out by Joy's mother calling out to her that supper was ready.

"Come on in girl and wash up." Joy heard her mother's voice sweep over the field and cross the broad ditch where she and Bubba were crawfishing. She lifted her fishing pole; a bamboo pole with a length of string tied to one end and a piece of meat to entice the little mudbugs on the other end and began to twirl the pole so that the string twisted around it. "I've got to go home Bubba. You best go home too."

"Aw come on Joy, you know you want me to go home 'cause you're scared I catch more crawfish than you," Bubba shot back. Joy turned around to give a smart answer but found him twirling his pole too. Acting like she didn't know that he was preparing to leave too, she bought into his line of joking. "I'm not scared of nothing Bubba and you know that. You know I can beat you at anything. You name it and I'll prove it." She bent down to gather her pail of clamoring crawfish and Bubba had his chance. He gave her a little shove causing her to lose her balance and he took off running, hollering over his shoulder, "I bet you can't beat me to the house." Joy quickly regained her balance, and in one movement picked up her bucket, grabbed her pole, and took off in a rapid dart. Although they were the same age she was smaller than Bubba and it didn't take her long to narrow the gap between them. He beat her to the driveway of his house by a split second, stuck his tongue out at her and waved good-bye. Joy reached her driveway gasping for breath but found enough to holler across the empty lot separating their houses, "Cheater, cheater chicken eater." She went into the house leaving her dreams back at the gully.

The smell of the chicken stew permeated the air in the small kitchen as Joy opened the screen door and let it slam behind her. "Mom, I'm home," she called as she entered the kitchen. Her father was already seated at the table belittling his wife for the way she looked while she placed silverware on the dinner table. Emily ignored her husband's remarks. He wasn't saying anything she hadn't heard before. She could never satisfy him anyway and lately she'd been much too tired to even try to make herself up anymore. Turning her attention to the joy of her life she exclaimed, "Lord almighty girl go wash up before you even think of sitting at my table." Her voice was stern but her eyes were gentle.

Joy made a quick turn from the table and all but ran to the kitchen sink. Before she could turn the water on, her mother called in exasperation, "Joy, how many times do I need to tell you, not at the kitchen sink. Go into the bathroom. Lord, I swear you act like you're five years old instead of ten." Joy shrugged her shoulders and headed for the bathroom shouting an apology over her shoulder.

"Emily, you really need to do something about that girl. You're much too soft on her. She's gonna grow up wild if you don't watch it." Her father hated the fact that Joy preferred running the gullies and woods with Bubba than staying by her mother and learning to do "girl" things. He hated that fact but remained far removed from assuming any responsibility for her behavior being content with blaming Emily for any and all of Joy's shortcomings.

Emily understood Joy's need to be away from the house. She wished she could be as free as Joy and roam the woods giving vent to the frustration she felt choking the life out of her instead of having to stay where her husband could see her at all times. She had to always be near the refrigerator so that when he called for a beer she could get one to him in a hurry. When Joy was anywhere around him, he stayed on her back hounding her about doing housework and not causing any trouble. If he had his way Joy would be doing her mother's work, freeing her mother to do his bidding.

Emily looked at her husband barely concealing her irritation with him. "Don't worry about Joy, she'll turn out just fine." Her mother knew Joy better than perhaps anyone else. Only ten years old, Joy was what some would call a tomboy, but inside of her was the biggest and softest heart anyone could hope to have. She had an understanding of people and a way of dealing with things that was beyond her years. Her mother might not have been able to give her a lot of material things, but this gift of understanding and getting through life, no matter the circumstances was of much greater value.

Joy returned to the table and for the most part they ate in silence. Only Joy with her keen observation noticed that Emily didn't eat much of anything. She had a way of pushing food around on her plate making it look like she'd eaten when in reality she'd consumed hardly anything. Joy had been noticing of late that her mother did not look well, but when she asked Emily about it, she always received the same answer of "everything's fine, there's nothing to worry about." Only tonight Joy sensed something different. Emily looked paler than usual. Joy could see beads of perspiration on her forehead, and for once Emily accepted Joy's offer to clear the supper table.

Joy hoped her mother could ease into a warm bath and perhaps rest a bit before going to bed, but that was not the case. Immediately upon rising from the supper table, her father began his demands on Emily. Joy pushed raging thoughts of what she'd like to do to her dad aside and began washing dishes vigorously pretending each dish was her father's face, while he gulped his favorite beer and Emily massaged his grubby feet.

Later that night Joy awoke to the sound of sobbing. Slipping quietly out of bed, she tiptoed to the living room. Her mother was crumpled on the floor next to the sofa, one arm extended toward the table with the phone on it. Trying not to panic, Joy ran to her mother's side. "Mom! Oh my God, Momma, please talk to me. What's wrong? What can I do?" The little girl knelt next to the most important person in her life and begged God to spare her mother. Emily tried hard to answer but nothing would come out except for garbled sobs. Swallowing her panic the frightened little girl grabbed the phone and dialed 911 then Bubba's phone number. Bubba's mother answered the phone and assured Joy that she would get help. Within minutes Bubba burst through Joy's front door still dressed in his pajamas.

He rushed to her side wanting to be there for the little girl that had shared everything with him for as long as he could remember. He'd always liked Joy's mother with her gentle eyes and soft voice but had never gotten close to her because of Joy's father. He never wanted Joy to have friends over so Joy had spent more time at his house than he had at hers. As they waited for his mother, he placed his arm around Joy's shoulders hoping he could somehow offer her some comfort. Remembering her courage he told her to be brave and to remember that she wasn't scared of anything.

She tore her gaze from her mother's beautiful face and looking at Bubba she said in a tight little voice, "I lied Bubba. I am scared of something. I'm scared my Momma's gonna die."

Bubba swallowed hard and said nothing. He couldn't. Joy had never shown vulnerability as she did at this moment. Suddenly as though time waited for this admission from Joy, they heard the sirens of the approaching ambulance.

As they picked Emily from the floor, Joy looked back at Bubba's mother and asked that she leave a note for her father. He wasn't home. She knew where to find him, but didn't really want to reach him. Joy knew that he wouldn't find the note until tomorrow, when he once again called out to Emily and she wouldn't respond. Then he would care. Not before. Joy's last thought as the ambulance pulled out of the driveway with her and her mother was to let the bastard drink. Let him choke in his vomit. She knew they'd be better off without him.

Bubba and his mother followed the ambulance in their car knowing that it would have been useless to try to persuade Joy to ride to the hospital with them. They knew about her stubbornness especially where her mother was concerned. They followed Joy into the lobby of the emergency room. As Bubba's mother took care of the admission, Joy sat in one of the cold plastic chairs. She was trying so hard to be grown up and adult like, sitting straight as an arrow in the hard chair. She sat there, moving nothing but her lips as she silently prayed like she'd never prayed before. Bubba ran up to her but was silenced when he saw the fear in her deep brown eyes. He sat next to her holding her icy hand while tears streamed down his freckled cheeks. He tried to imagine himself in Joy's place but the fear and pain those thoughts brought to him were too great, so he just sat there praying to the all-loving God they were taught about in religion class and every now and then he'd squeeze Joy's cold little hand, never getting any response from her.

Finally, after what seemed like years, the doctor emerged from the doors marked Emergency Personnel Only. He looked around taking in the sight of the little girl with the pale face and unruly brown hair and the freckle faced little boy sitting next to her then his gaze locked on Bubba's mother. At the doctor's nod, she walked over to him. The doctor and Bubba's mom turned their backs to the children and placed their heads together. They spoke in muted whispers for a few minutes then Joy saw the doctor shake his head from side to side. She watched as in slow motion Bubba's mother turned and started walking toward her, her face wet with tears. She could feel the panic rise in her as the realization came to her. Internally she screamed denial. Her mother could not be dead. Her mother would never die and leave her alone with her drunken father. Her beautiful mother would walk through those emergency doors any minute. Joy turned her gaze from Bubba's mother to the swinging emergency doors. Shock took over the small frame as a smile replaced the thinly drawn lines of her lips and a look of expectant joy replaced the fear in her eyes. She jumped up from her seat, breaking the hold Bubba had on her hand, and started running toward the emergency doors before Bubba's mom could get to her. In a dream-like state, she heard the dreaded words, "No, Joy don't go in there. She's gone. Sweetheart your mother is dead."

In her head the words were muted, softly sobbed but outside the wounded child's voice pierced the quietness of the late night corridors as she wailed the sorrowful cry of grief, screaming the word no repeatedly until she crumpled to the floor in an unconscious heap.

The day of the funeral was beautiful. Crisp blue skies dotted with small puffy white clouds covered the small group of people that came to say their final good-byes to Emily. Joy was snuggled between Bubba and his mother, her small face still pale but now with a determined look to it. She had shed no more tears since the night she'd admitted to Bubba that she was scared. She watched it all. She heard it all. She stood and watched as her father sobbed and wailed that he could not go on without his Emily. She shuddered as she caught the hatred in his eyes as he stared at her across her mother's casket. She saw the pall bearers place their boutonnieres on her mother's casket and watched as the priest gave the crucifix that had graced the inside cover of Emily's casket to her father. She gave very little notice as the priest extended his hand to her and offered words of comfort. It didn't matter anymore. Her mother was dead, her father hated her and nothing mattered. She was by herself now and she'd make it.

She smiled to herself as she imagined her mother telling her one more time that if life handed you lemons you had better make lemonade. So lemonade she would make and you could bet your booty, it would be the best damn lemonade anyone ever tasted. She straightened her small shoulders and walked away from where her mother lay. She still had her father to face then life would be splendid, if you could define splendid as being lonely and scared.

She didn't know what was in store for her and never suspected what she received. Life with her father was sheer hell. Joy had little time to herself anymore. Gone were the days she and Bubba had spent crawfishing and hiking in the woods. Now her time was taken up with chores meant for someone much older than she, but there was no one else to do them. The hardest part was finding something to cook. Her father spent most of his time and most of the money on booze. Most of the time he drank at home and these were the times Joy hated the most. He would make her sit across from him and listen while he cursed her out and blamed her for her mother's death. The once playful, energetic little tomboy slowly turned into a thin, withdrawn little girl.

Life dragged on and a month before Joy's eleventh birthday, while she was home alone asleep in her room an intruder entered the house. Joy awoke to the sound of breaking glass. Sleepily she got out of bed and walked out into the hall taking the man by surprise. Opening her mouth to scream, she froze. No sound came from the little girl. The man panicked. He shoved Joy down on the floor and took off running. The little girl's eyes were big as saucers and she couldn't believe her luck when she saw him run out of the house. Shakily she arose from the floor and called Bubba. He came over and convinced her she needed to call the police. Being a child and not thinking of the consequences of having the police find out that she'd been left alone, not for the first time, she took his advice and dialed 911. In minutes the police were at her house. After looking around and finding the broken window where the man had entered the house they sat Joy down and began asking questions. By this time Bubba had called his mother and she'd come running to be by Joy's side. When the officers heard that Joy was often left alone while her father visited the neighborhood bar they concluded that it would be in her best interest if they removed her from her father's custody. Shocked and not knowing what was to become of her, Joy just sat there, looking lost.

Bubba's mom told the police where they might find Joy's father. She packed some of Joy's clothing promising to pack and send her the rest of her things once she found out where Joy would be. She handed Joy the bag then hugged the thin frame of the little girl she loved like her own. "I would take her myself officer," she sobbed, Abut I can hardly afford to raise my little boy." Saying goodbye to Joy was one of the hardest things she'd ever done. The only thing that was harder was watching her son and his best friend part. Bubba was openly crying, not even trying to check his tears as they poured from his eyes. His last words to Joy as the officers took her from her house were happy birthday because he knew in his gut that he would never see her again.

Joy was brought to a shelter for abused children. She remained quite and withdrawn, eating very little and sitting there dry-eyed. She'd speak only when she was spoken to saying only what it took to answer the questions directed toward her. At night, she'd hug her knees to her bony little chest and pray that God take her home to her momma. When her eyes would open the next morning, she'd compel herself to another day of existence. She shielded herself from any feelings. Good or bad. Thoughts of her father never entered her mind and she pushed any thoughts of Bubba and her past so far to the rear of her mind that it would be years before she'd ever be able to face them.

Two weeks after being brought to the shelter, she was summoned to the interview room. It seemed there was a family who wanted to meet her. Joy stood in front of the Taylors as she was questioned as to whether or not she would like to live with them. Not caring who she lived with and thinking maybe it would be best to try to go on with her life, she nodded yes. They arranged to pick her up the next day.

The Taylors lived in a small community thirty miles east of Baton Rouge. Their house was modest and very clean. They were quick to lay down rules and make their expectations known to Joy. She would be expected to help with the cleaning and the cooking. It wasn't anything that she wasn't used to so she gladly did what she was told. Having the responsibility of running a household taken off of her frail shoulders, Joy found a measure of peace in doing her part of the housework. Eventually she relaxed and began to trust the Taylors. They introduced her to their friends as their little girl and their children, all grown, accepted her as one of the family. Vulnerable as she was, Joy reluctantly opened her heart to the Taylors and gave them some of her much guarded love.

Relieved of the past, Joy soon blossomed under the care of the Taylors. Her once frail and bony frame began to fill out and hinted of the beauty that was to come with maturity. She soon became a familiar face in the neighborhood often seen helping the senior citizens with the shopping or errands. Once she began to trust again, her winsome smile returned and all it took was one look from her big soft brown eyes and immediately you wanted to become her friend, however she never allowed anyone to replace Bubba in her heart. Some of her carefree ways returned as she followed Pop Taylor on fishing expeditions and helped him with the yard work.

The years sped by and almost overnight Joy became a young woman. She turned fourteen and all of a sudden, she was too grown up to go fishing with Pop Taylor and instead wanted to spend all of her time trying out new hair styles and make-up. Popular with both boys and girls a lot of her time was taken up with friends. Life became normal. More normal than she'd ever experienced, even with her biological family.

Then all hell broke loose. One day she came home from school to find Mrs. Taylor crying. When she asked her what was wrong, she was promptly admonished that it was none of her business. Suddenly there was a shortage of household funds. Pop Taylor began coming home later and later as the weeks passed. Tensions in the Taylor home were running high. Mom Taylor never spoke anymore, all she did was yell. She started taking out her hostilities and frustrations on Joy, finding fault with every little error Joy made. She accused her of unbelievable things. She took away privileges, and Joy found herself grounded weekly. As if overnight, Joy became an intruder instead of one of the family.

She could have handled that, but the hell her foster father put her through was another thing. He began sexually harassing her nightly. To keep her quiet about his visits to her, he threatened that if she made his propositions known to his wife or to anyone, he would convince them that she had come on to him. So she'd kept quiet, hoping he would tire of his game and leave her alone. But without fail, he would show up in her room sometimes minutes after saying goodnight and sometimes hours later.

She defended herself against him as best she could and had managed to prevent him from getting what he wanted. As his advances grew more forceful she had to revert to more resourceful means of warding him off. One night she went to bed prepared. When he paid his nightly visit to her, she pulled an ice pick from under her pillow and threatened to stick it in him if he didn't leave her alone. It worked. He left and Joy spent the rest of the night wide-awake with the ice pick clutched tightly in her hands.

The next morning she packed her clothes and left, leaving behind a note to the Taylors saying if they contacted the state officials she would tell them of the abuse she had suffered at their hands.

Shuddering, she sobbed, "have you ever lost someone you'd placed all your confidence and love in?" Looking at Shaze imploringly she asked, "do you know how much it hurts to be betrayed by someone you believe in so much? Oh, Shaze," she cried, burying her head in her hands, "I don't know what made them change toward me, like that. I suppose I'll never understand why it happened."

Shaze took her face between his hands and barely able to stand the hurt and bewildered look in her eyes, placed a tender kiss on her forehead while gently pushing her head against his shoulder.

"Sick bastard," he muttered, patting Joy's head as one would pat a baby.

Between broken breaths, she stammered, "maybe I caused them to hate me. Somehow, I must've done something to make them turn on me." As though obtaining a revelation, she sat upright in her seat and grabbed Shaze's arm, "do you think it's possible? Could I've possibly caused these people some shame? Some reason to hate me?"

Shaze's voice was adamant as he tried to rid her of the guilt she was obviously feeling as he quickly reassured her, "Uh uh! No way. There is no way in this world that someone like you can be responsible for those people's actions. Take that thought out of your mind now. Do you hear me? Those people were sick and the state should never have placed you in their care."

With eyes full of trust and gratitude, she tried to regain her composure as she continued. Frightened and alone, she had tried not to panic. With the help of one of her friends she found a safe place to store her clothes in the family's storage shed. She'd sleep at one friend's house one night and at another's the next night. Some nights she had no place to go. Those were the nights she really had to fight the memories of better times. The longing for better days was almost too much to bear.

Eventually, the state caught up with her and took her into custody again. This time they found her a home with a young couple in New Orleans. Skeptical at first, Joy shied away from a relationship with her new family but fortunately for Joy, they had been informed of her past and persevered in their attempts at friendship.

They had just found out that they would never have children of their own. Filled with regret at their failure to conceive a child, they nevertheless wanted more than anything a child to lavish love and affection on. The fact that Joy was a teenager did not deter them.

They agreed with the social worker that placed Joy with them that she needed to be with someone that could provide friendship while nurturing trust in adults. Once Joy laid to rest the suspicions she harbored against all adults, a strong bond developed between her and her new family. They were a good Christian family and sooner than she expected Joy felt like she belonged. She'd found home. With the love the Brackens showered her with, she was soon herself again. It was while living with the Brackens that her life took on meaning.

"How long did you live with them?" Shaze asked as he noticed her relaxing somewhat as these happier memories flooded her mind.

"I moved out when I turned eighteen. I hated the idea of having to leave them, but they had fulfilled their duties and were planning to move to Texas and the state had stopped paying for my care. I was a senior in high school then and was engaged to Ryan. His parents offered to take me in, and I accepted."

"When was the last time you heard from your foster parents?"

Joy swallowed a sob, "two days after they left New Orleans, I read in a newspaper that they had been killed in an automobile accident. Their car apparently stalled on a Houston freeway, causing a terrible pile up. They died instantly."

A wistful look came into her eyes. "Why do you think things like that happen to good people?" Her question went unanswered as Shaze lowered his gaze and rearranged himself in his seat. Clearing his throat he broke the momentary silence her question had caused between them, and then he asked, "How did you meet Ryan?"

A smile touched her lips as she gave life to the memory of the event that changed her life. "My first day at Franklin High, I was walking down the hall looking for my Trig class. Intent on getting to class on time, I walked right between the two best looking guys in school. My arms caught theirs causing them to drop their books and mine went flying everywhere. Gosh, I remember it like it was yesterday." A touch of longing crept into her voice and Shaze saw her eyes light up as she remembered her first encounter with Ryan.

He felt a stab of jealousy shoot through his body. Come on, Shaze, you can't be jealous of a dead lover, he rebuked himself.

"Can't you picture me, standing there, looking up at the two most gorgeous guys I'd ever seen?" Laughing at the image the memory evoked, she continued, "I must've looked really stupid, standing there with my red face and tears of humiliation rolling down my cheeks.

Ryan and Hank looked at me then looked at each other and burst out laughing. I remember trying to apologize and failing miserably as nothing but rambling sounds came out. Wishing the floor would open up and swallow me, I had turned to run away when Ryan reached out and caught my arm. It was love at first touch," she laughed.

"From that day until the day I married Ryan, the three of us were inseparable. We quickly became known around campus as the "trio.""

"Didn't you and Ryan find it somewhat inconvenient having a third party tag along with you all of the time?" Shaze's voice held a hint of jealousy and something else, which Joy could not identify.

"Not really. We were so much a part of each other; it didn't feel right when one was missing. We used to laugh and say that we would have the first three party marriage in history. Husband, wife and spare." Smiling, she reached up and wiped a tear as it escaped from her eye and trailed down her cheek.

"You know, you're right. It does feel better sharing these memories with someone," she said. A feeling of freedom permeated her mind as she relinquished her hold on the memories she'd kept locked up for so long. The door to freedom, however, did not stay open long as his next question thrust a knife deep into her heart and she remembered why she'd kept the door to her memories locked. Facing them was too painful!

"How long were you married to Ryan? You obviously loved each other a great deal. What ended the marriage?" Shaze was becoming merciless as he questioned Joy.

Naked pain swam in her eyes as she looked up at him.

"Death ended it." Her answer was a hoarse whisper wrenched from the depths of her existence. "We waited and planned two years for that night. Our plans were filled with love and life but reality served us death and division."

"Oh, my sweet baby. What hell you must've gone through. How did he die, can you tell me more?" His voice held an edge of urgency as he prodded Joy for details.

Arriving at the point in her memory where intense pain still held her prisoner, she lowered her head into her hands.

Placing an arm around her shaking shoulders, Shaze tried to comfort her but knew the pain was too deep to reach. For a brief moment remorse for what he made her go through, touched his heart, but with a subtle mental flick of his hand, he brushed it away.

Had Joy not been so consumed by the sobs claiming her senses, she would have grown concerned at the underlying tone in Shaze's voice as he asked her about the details of Ryan's death.

Raising her head Joy took a deep ragged breath, "I still don't know what happened." The cry coming from the anguished woman provided Shaze a glimpse of the hell that had haunted her for years. Her brow furrowed as she struggled with the memories.

In a dreamlike state and with a faltering voice she relived her last moments with Ryan. "It was storming. We finished taking the wedding pictures and I remember Hank kissing us goodbye. He was leaving for basic training immediately after the ceremony. I threw my bouquet into the crowd, and then Ryan and I ran out of the building. Everyone was laughing and throwing rice at us. Ryan opened the door of the car for me." Joy narrowed her eyes like she was trying to focus on the image in her mind. "I remember seeing lightning streak across the sky as I slid across the seat making room for Ryan. Slipping behind the steering wheel, he leaned over and kissed me." Her voice grew faint as though speaking from a great distance and she said slowly as she relived the scene, "he placed the key in the ignition and turned it. Just then a crack of thunder sounded and that was the last thing I remember. My next lucid moment was when I came to, lying in a hospital bed, two weeks later. I called out for Ryan. Instead of him coming to my bedside, his parents came. When I asked why I was in a hospital, they told me of the accident. They gave me the information they had. For some unexplained reason, the car had blown up when Ryan turned the key in the ignition. I asked again for Ryan. The pain in their eyes confirmed my worst fears. Ryan was dead. Killed instantly, they told me."

Joy's face was ravaged with pain as she turned her head away from Shaze and gazed through the window. She began trembling as her words brought home to her once again, the fact that the man she loved more than life itself, was dead.

Shaze hugged her close to him. "It's okay, love. That was all in the past and it can't hurt you anymore. I won't let it."

Placing her confidence in what Shaze said, Joy relaxed a little, placed her head on his shoulder and fell into an exhausted sleep.

While Joy was reliving her past, Shaze had thoughts of his own. His heart broke when he envisioned Joy as a frightened young girl fighting for her virginity. When he saw her small hands clinch into fists, he pictured the ice pick clutched in her hands and when he saw a soft dreamy look come into her eyes during periods of silence, he felt a stab of jealousy shoot through his body. Remorse for what she'd gone through nagged at him, but with a subtle mental flick of his hand he'd brush it away. His feelings were a mixture of elation and sadness. He was elated that his plan had succeeded, but at the same time he felt saddened that Joy had to get caught in the cross fire.

Poor little thing, he thought. She has been through so much that could have been avoided. It was too bad that she had chosen Ryan instead of the other one. Joy didn't deserve the hell she had gone through because of her love for Ryan. Shaze looked lovingly down at the sleeping woman. The early morning sunrise shed a gentle beam of light on her face causing the tears that squeezed through her closed eyes to sparkle with a beauty of their own. With a heart full of sorrow and a touch filled with tenderness, he wiped her cheeks. Touching his finger to his lips, he followed the path her tears had taken, ending on the scar that ran down the side of her face near her hairline. A scar he was just as responsible for as the accident was. You're treading on dangerous ground, Shaze old buddy, he told himself. This was not in his original plans. Love had no place in this deal. He could not let genuine love for this woman interfere with the plan.

He still didn't know what this trip held for Joy or for him. Suspecting the old man was dying, and knowing the old lady had died a few years ago, he felt confident that Joy's being called back had something to do with an inheritance. A sizable inheritance according to his sources. The old man was a jewel magnate, owning a chain of jewelry stores throughout the country.

Shaze had stood back in the shadows and watched one store grow into two and two into three. He watched from a distance, never venturing close enough to be noticed. How he longed to approach the old man for a job. Any job! He would have gladly settled for even the most menial of tasks, but two things had kept him away. One was fear of being recognized and the other was pride. He didn't need to be the "work boy" for this man while Ryan was the "prince" of everything. It was this latter reason that spurred his vengeance on. He had become the nemesis of the Young family.

Shaze was pulled back to the present as the pilot's voice announced their approach to the New Orleans airport.

Joy began to stir and awaken from her troubled sleep as she heard the pilot's voice. A few minutes later she was welcomed to New Orleans by a stewardess as she stepped into the cool, busy interior of the airport.

Sighing, she thought perhaps things wouldn't be as hard as she imagined them to be. Face it Joy, she chided herself, this can't be as bad as it was the last time you were here. Her departure from this airport years ago had been one of the hardest things she'd ever done.

Joy squared her shoulders, took a deep breath and said in a voice, which sounded more confident than she felt, "Well, let's see why I got called back home." She picked up her overnight case and walked out into the haziness of a hot and humid New Orleans morning, with Shaze following closely behind her.

# CHAPTER 3

$B$oth Joy and Shaze were quiet on the ride from the airport, causing a deathlike silence to fall between them. Consternation over what she would find once she arrived at the hospital had Joy deep in thought, and Shaze was desperately trying to come up with some plausible reason to stay behind while she conducted her business.

Opening their mouths to speak at the same time, they burst into nervous laughter instead. Thankful for the break in the tension-filled car, Joy hesitantly asked Shaze if he would like to go on to the hotel and secure rooms for both of them while she went to the hospital.

Perceiving her discomfort at having him with her, Shaze assured her that would be the best way of handling things. Without knowing it, Joy had solved his problem of risking recognition while coming up with the solution to her problem. Shaze tapped the cab driver on the shoulder and told him to drop him off at Le Pavillon Hotel. It felt like a thousand pound weight had been lifted from his shoulders once he gave the hotel name to the cabby, so relieved was he to be spared going to the hospital with Joy. He stood on the curb in front of the hotel and watched as the cab pulled away toward the hospital, hoping his suspicions about the inheritance were true.

The ride to the hospital was much too fast for Joy. In what seemed like seconds to her, they arrived and she had to leave the safe confines of the cab. With trembling legs and sweating palms she walked through the doors marked Emergency Only. The morning shift was preparing to start their day's work as Joy opened her handbag and pulled out the piece of paper she'd written Charles's room number on. Trying to convince herself she was doing the right thing, she stepped into the elevator and pushed the button indicating the ninth floor.

Stepping out of the elevator into the quiet corridor, Joy paused a minute and looked around her. The antiseptic smell, the quietness and the muted colors of the decor were all too familiar. She stood there, the tears stinging her eyes as she struggled to hold the past in check.

Just then a nurse saw her and began to walk toward her. Joy wiped her eyes with the back of her hand as she greeted the nurse.

"Hi, I'm Joy Young. I was contacted concerning Mr. Charles Young. Is he all right? Is Dr. Peters still here?"

The nurse could see the tension and worry in Joy and quickly assured her that Charles was resting in his room and that she would page Dr. Peters to let him know she had arrived.

Thanking the nurse, Joy started toward Charles's room. She had taken only a couple of steps when her knees buckled. She reached out, clutching the wall as she sought to steady herself. The nurse ran to her side. "Ms. Young, are you all right?"

"I'm fine, thank you," Joy responded with a shaky voice.

"Excuse me for saying so Ms. Young, but you don't seem fine. Would you like to sit for a minute and catch your breath?" The nurse held Joy's elbow and looked at her with a worried look.

Joy declined the nurse's offer, thinking to herself that the longer she prolonged the meeting, the harder it would be. Pulling herself together again, Joy walked to the room. She paused at the door, but only for a moment of silent prayer for courage, then purposefully pushed the heavy hospital door open.

The beeping and hissing sounds of the equipment hooked up to Charles assaulted her ears first. Adjusting her eyes to the dimness of the room, she let out a gasp.

Although she hadn't known what to expect, she certainly had not expected what her eyes beheld. She was in no way prepared for the scene that she now faced. Monitors and tubes seemed to be everywhere. From her position near the door it seemed that he had stopped breathing but the beeping of the monitor told her otherwise.

She tiptoed to the bedside and saw that he was sleeping. So, is this what they call "resting?" How in the hell can one rest with all of this going on?, Joy thought as she looked down at the dying man surrounded by machines and filled with tubes entering and leaving his body at various points. Slowly, so as not to cause a disturbance, she lowered herself into the chair next to the bed and took a good look at the man who was once her father-in-law.

The years had not been kind to him. He had aged considerably in the past seven years. Charles had always been a very nice looking man. Powerful and energetic, his demeanor demanded attention upon entering a room. Now, his once robust frame seemed fragile and emaciated. Looking closely, Joy could see loosely hanging flesh had replaced the once well-built muscles. His thick chestnut hair had thinned and become streaked with gray.

Sitting and watching Charles, Joy reflected on the fragility of life. This was something she had thought about often. In an instant, all one's strength and power can be usurped, leaving but an empty shell. This thought had become a realization during her recuperation from the accident.

One minute she and Ryan had been laughing, full of life and love and the next minute everything was gone. All gone. Ryan had been taken away and she had been left a shell of the woman she had been.

Life was all too fragile, she thought as she gently picked up Charles's wrinkled hand. Bowing her head and closing her eyes, she whispered a prayer on his behalf. Opening her eyes, her heart jumped. Charles was looking intently at her with faded blue eyes. He had awakened and taken advantage of her bowed head to study her.

Smiling, Joy leaned down near him. "Hello, Charles. It's been some time hasn't it?" She watched as he attempted a feeble smile in return. Joy saw his lips move and knew he was trying to say something, but she could not hear what he was saying. Trying to comfort him she said, "Shhh. It's okay Charles. I'm here now. Just relax and try to get more rest."

Charles's eyes grew large and a look of desperation fell on his face. He began to frantically convey something else, but Joy still could not make out what he was trying to tell her. "Charles, I'm here," she repeated hoping to calm him down. "I'm not going anywhere. I promise I'll be here when you wake up," she tried to quiet him with reassurance thinking he might be frightened she'd leave. This did not appease him. His state was rapidly becoming more agitated. Frightened, Joy reached for the call button to summon the nurse, but paused as she heard the door opening. Turning she saw Dr. Peters enter the room.

"Ms. Young?"

"Oh, Dr. Peters! Thank God, you're here. I don't know what to do. He's determined to tell me something and I've tried to understand, but I just can't make it out. I'm afraid my being here is doing more damage than good."

Joy blasted the doctor with words laden with fear. Her trembling lips just barely allowed the words to escape, but the doctor heard enough to know that she was nearly hysterical.

Motioning her to the door, Dr. Peters placed his hands on her shoulders. "Take a deep breath, Ms. Young. Relax. Charles is a desperate man right now. I'm afraid he knows he's dying and is feeling an urgency to speak to you before it's too late."

"What is this urgent message that he needs to tell me, Dr. Peters?"

Taking Joy's arm he guided her to Charles's bedside. Looking down at his life-long friend he comforted the dying man. "Charles, are you in any pain?" The words were so softly spoken Joy had to strain to hear them. Charles shook his head indicating that he wasn't, but the doctor knew differently. This man was in a great deal of pain, physically as well as emotionally. The show of courage and strength the old man was displaying by holding on this long awed Dr. Peters. He knew that Charles's need to speak to Joy fueled his determination to stay alive.

Dr. Peters knew the reason for the urgency that his patient was feeling and he could see that the solemnity of it all was alarming Joy.

She watched as the doctor leaned down near Charles, and whispered in his ear. She could see Charles relax as the doctor's words immediately put him at ease. Joy smiled her thanks to the doctor and he returned her smile with one that was weighty with sorrow and regret. Joy noted the tears glimmering in his eyes as he straightened up and looked at her.

"Charles knows that his time is running out Joy and he has held up this long because he has something to say to you."

Joy looked expectantly first at the doctor and then at Charles. She watched as Charles blinked and tears began to roll down his sunken cheeks. He inhaled and she could see how hard it was for him to breathe. Leaning over his bony body Joy tenderly asked him what it was that he had to tell her. She felt his cold, bony fingers try to tighten around hers as he whispered, "I'm sorry. We thought we were doing what was right. Can you please forgive me?"

Before Joy could respond, she felt his body shudder and his fingers release their hold of hers as his lifeless hand fell to the bed. Her head jerked up as she focused on the monitor and saw that it was flat-lining. Joy reluctantly stepped away from the bed as Doctor Peters rushed to the bedside and checked Charles's pulse.

With tears blurring her vision, Joy watched as Dr. Peters gently closed Charles's eyes. He turned to face her and Joy could see the sorrow he was feeling at the loss of his friend. Walking to her side, he placed his hands on her shoulders. "I'm sorry. He's gone," he said and pulled her to him in a fatherly embrace. Then gripping her elbow, he guided her out of the room.

Once outside the room, Dr. Peters invited Joy to join him in a cup of coffee. He still had business to take care of. Charles had thankfully lived long enough to apologize to Joy and now the rest was up to him and Charles's attorney.

They sat at a table in a far corner of the hospital cafeteria where he hoped they would not be disturbed. He took Joy's hand in his and told her of the friendship he and Charles had shared. He recounted to her of their times together, mostly on the golf course, where she had often been the topic of their conversation.

Joy listened; her hands wrapped around the steaming mug of coffee, as Dr. Peters told her Charles had viewed her as a daughter received through a marriage that had not been given a chance. A fact that had caused the man much dismay. He had often conveyed his worry about her to Dr. Peters. More than once he had told the doctor how much he regretted not keeping in touch with her over the years. But he'd felt it would be best if they severed all ties so that she would not stay tied to her past. She was still so young and had her life before her.

"But, is that what he wanted to tell me?" she asked the doctor. "It somehow feels like there has to be more to it," she muttered half to him and half to herself.

The doctor didn't acknowledge her question. Instead, he fulfilled his last promise made to his dear friend.

"Ms Young, may I call you Joy?"

Joy answered his question with a nod.

"Charles wanted me to inform you of a few things upon the event of his death. He would like you to go to his house. Stay there while you're in town, if you like. In his desk drawer you will find an envelope with your name on it. I know it's there because I put it there myself. Charles had me take it from his safe yesterday. There you will find the name of his attorney. You're to contact him and make an appointment with him. He will help you with the rest." Looking at his watch Dr. Peters stood up and extended a hand toward Joy. "I haven't had the time to tell you how good it is to see you again. I'm just so sorry that it has to be under these circumstances. If you need me for anything, I want you to know that I can be by your side within minutes of being summoned. Please remember that."

Joy stood and took the extended hand offered her. "Thank you Dr. Peters. You've been a big help to me already, although I still don't know what's happened. Everything is moving so quickly and I'm having a hard time putting it together. I surely didn't expect Charles to look so different. He's aged so much and...oh, my God, I've completely forgotten...what about Mrs. Young? Where is she? Why isn't she here?"

"Mamie died two years ago." The doctor and friend of the Youngs answered the question he saw mirrored in Joy's eyes. "Cancer," he said. "Her death really took a toll on Charles. You know, those two absolutely doted on each other."

Suddenly Joy began to tremble all over, as shock at what she was hearing began to set in. "First it was Ryan, then Mamie and now Charles," she whispered as she realized how much everything had changed in the time that she'd been gone. She felt twinges of guilt because she had not tried to keep in touch with them after the accident. After all, they had been so good to her.

Dr. Peters gently placed an arm around her small, trembling shoulders and pressed her head against his chest. "Cry, little one," he whispered to her. She had been so brave to come back here. Her life had been a rough one, she'd had to fight harder than anyone he'd ever known, and her battles weren't over yet. She was about to face the hardest battle she would ever have to fight. Dr. Peters let out a sigh. His job of telling her what to do was so minor compared to the job the attorney still faced.

His gentle touch and soft voice tore down the barriers of strength she had erected for protection. She allowed her head to rest against his chest as she gave in to the sobs that had threatened to claim her since Dr. Peters had closed Charles's eyes. After a few minutes of intense crying and finally being able to control herself, she reluctantly pulled away from the comforting arms of the doctor. "Thank you again, Dr. Peters. May I leave now, or is there something I need to take care of…you know…with Charles dead…do I need to sign anything or…"

"Don't worry about anything, Joy. Just go home. I mean to wherever you're staying. Do you have a place to stay, or are you going to stay at Charles's? Are you by yourself?" Genuine concern for her filled his voice.

Suddenly remembering Shaze, Joy answered the doctor's last question. "No, I'm not alone Dr. Peters. I brought a friend with me from Los Angeles."

"Good, find your friend. You shouldn't be alone now. I'll take care of things here. Just do what I told you. Okay?" He hugged Joy and walked away.

She wiped her eyes, blew her nose, picked up her handbag and went in search of a phone to call Shaze.

Shaze, eager to find out what happened, met Joy at the door of his hotel room. Hugging her and then pulling away he looked deeply into her eyes. Oh, talk to me. Tell me what I want to hear. His mind screamed out to her. His curiosity was getting the best of him. He just had to know what happened. It had been hell sitting here in this miserable room waiting. And he hated waiting. I've waited long enough, he thought. But he had to tread softly; he couldn't push or seem too anxious. Seeing the distressed look in her eyes he felt sorry for the woman who stood in front of him. Damn, here I go again. Softening up, and I can't afford to do that, Shaze cautioned himself.

"Love, are you all right?" he asked her, filling his voice with concern. "Can you tell me what happened? Is the old man still alive?" Before she could respond to his questions he caught the confused look in her eyes. Trying to cover his tracks, he pulled her to him.

"Hey, what am I thinking about? You don't need to talk to me about this right now. I'm sorry, Love. You must've gone through hell today. Let me run a hot bath for you. Would you like me to call room service for a cup of tea or a drink maybe?"

Waving away his suggestions, Joy replied, "Shaze, it's all right. I'm okay. Look, I think I'll go back to my room. I need to be by myself for a little while. I'll talk to you later. Okay?" Tiptoeing she kissed him lightly on the cheek. Turning to walk out of the room she caught a glimpse of the dark look that ran across his face.

While Joy was resting in her room and getting her thoughts together, Shaze was pacing in his room. The dark look Joy had briefly glimpsed was now in full bloom. His eyes grew hard and his face became distorted with the anger he was feeling inside. I knew it! I knew this place was bad luck, he fumed. We're not here twenty-four hours yet, and she's already pulling away from me. Well it's not going to happen. Do you hear me, you old bastard? You're not going to take her away from me. He cursed brutally into the stillness of his room, while shaking his fist in the air.

Working himself into a frenzied state he gave no thought to how he would explain his anger to Joy if need arose. Picking up the phone, he ordered a bottle of bourbon from room service. Loosening his tie he continued to give vent to the rebellious feelings surging to the surface and spilling forth in his actions, resulting in his kicking a chair over before dropping to his knees in sobs.

Joy ran herself a hot bath and added the bubbling bath beads the hotel supplied for the comfort of its patrons. Lying there she allowed her mind to roam and the happenings of the day to soak in. There was so much to think about. The thing that bothered her most was the look she had seen in Shaze's eyes and the urgency she'd heard in his voice as he asked her what had happened. She'd never heard that urgency in him before. It sounded more than urgent. It had insistence. Like his whole life hinged on what her answers would be. Suddenly she felt a trail of icy fingers run down her spine and a sense of fear even more intense than the fear she'd felt in coming home.

Joy reluctantly left the soothing bath, dried herself off and decided to order a light dinner from room service. She just couldn't face Charles's house tonight. She figured she'd get a good night's sleep, if that were possible, and tackle the house and whatever was in store for her tomorrow. Dinner came. Joy picked at it, scarcely touching it, half expecting Shaze to call her. The call never came and she didn't make an effort to call him. Both went to bed late that night in each their own hell.

Early the next morning, a contrite and hung over Shaze called Joy's room. He asked about her night and asked if she had slept peacefully. He tried to reassure her of his love for her and felt that he fell short of convincing her. His anxiety mounted as he heard her tell him that Charles had died shortly after her arrival at the hospital the day before. She told him what Dr. Peters told her about going to Charles's house and about the instructions he had given to her. With this news Shaze threw caution to the wind and offered to go with her to the house. Although she needed his support, she declined his offer, telling him that this was something she had to do by herself. She knew the house held many memories of Ryan and she needed to handle these alone.

Shaze again felt a stab of jealousy but did not push her into changing her mind. He told her he'd be at the hotel waiting for her if she needed him. Thanking him she hung up the phone. Only then did he realize she never mentioned loving him or that she missed him. He could feel the cold fingers of doubt circle his heart and heard the inner voice of his mind telling him it had already started. He was losing her. Again, he vowed to the dead Charles that he, Shaze, would win this time. The old man had nothing left with which to fight him. His only weapon, Ryan, was long dead and now the old man was gone too. Shaze was afraid only of the living, not of the dead.

# CHAPTER 4

❀

*J*oy hailed a cab and gave the driver an address on St. Charles Avenue. Seeing the look in the cabby's eyes, Joy at once regretted leaving the rental with Shaze.

The cabby was bold in his scrutiny of her. "That's a mighty nice place you're going to. Got business in that area?" he asked, while smacking away at his gum. "Ain't that old man Young's place? How's the old codger, anyways?" He looked at Joy from his rear view mirror. She stared back, silent as a stone. Probably cold as a damn stone too, thought the cabby, as he flicked the meter on and drove away.

Joy leaned back in the seat. Just my luck, she muttered under her breath, you'd know it, of all the cab drivers in New Orleans; I would get one that likes to talk. To top it all off, he seemed to know Charles. That he knew Charles surprised her. It really shouldn't have because Charles had friends in all walks of life.

Had it been in any other situation, Joy would have spoken to the cab driver; she would have told him that Charles had passed away, but things being the way they were, anxiety and excitement replaced her usual friendliness. What would she find in Charles's desk? Why an apology? Last night her sleep had been interrupted repeatedly by the image of Charles asking for forgiveness. He'd done nothing to upset her. Perhaps in his sickened state, he'd imagined offending her and that was the reason behind the apology. Ending her speculation, she told herself she'd just have to wait and see what she'd find.

Forcing herself to relax and enjoy the ride she noticed the surroundings began to look familiar and she let the memories they stirred up rise within her. She gave the memories full reign of her senses and was glad that the cab driver didn't seem hurried.

They drove by the local teen hangout where Ryan had given her his ring. It wasn't his class ring, but a woven tri-colored band. Ryan was so proud of this ring because he had designed it. He'd often told Joy that she was his first love and second in line was his love for jewelry designing. Joy smiled as she envisioned his face the day he gave her the ring. He'd had so much pride shining from his eyes. He'd laughed when Joy remarked about the pride and he'd come back quickly with the comment, "I'd be a fool not to be proud. I have everything a man could want. I have the best girl in Louisiana and my future planned. There aren't many of us that can boast of that." Joy had hugged him tightly then proceeded to tickle him, which led to a mock wrestling match whereby Ryan had fallen out of the car in front of many of their friends. Joy could still hear herself laughing and telling her friends that she now had him where she wanted him. At her feet! Everyone had begun to tease Ryan then and all had a good time because of it.

Then the cab passed in front of the park where she and Ryan had planned their wedding. She was tempted to ask the cab driver to stop so she could sit on the swing where they had named all their future children. They had wanted four. Neither wanted just one. They'd agreed being an only child wasn't the best way of life. They didn't want their children growing up never experiencing sibling fights and the closeness of sharing secrets that children from a large family often experienced. Oh, Ryan, we had so much to look forward to, she thought with a wistful smile on her lips. A smile that never quite reached her eyes.

A little further down the road she spotted the car dealership where she and Ryan had strolled on weekends looking for the perfect car. They had spotted the silver Jaguar simultaneously and he had challenged her in a race to the car. She could remember the excitement surrounding him as he later described the car to his father. This car had been his graduation gift from his parents. They had given him full control in the choice of the car as a reward for being an honor graduate and a son they had every right to be proud of. Charles had jokingly told Ryan that he had lucked out, because if he had seen the car first, it would have been his. Ryan had laughed and affectionately slapped his daddy on the back. They had been more like good buddies than father and son. That was one thing Joy had liked so much about Ryan's family. They'd always treated both she and Ryan as equals instead of like children.

Up to now the memories were bittersweet, bringing a smile to her lips and a burden of sorrow to her heart. As they turned the corner Joy took in a sharp breath as she faced the church where she and Ryan were married. The memories became more vivid and the pain more intense as she looked further down the road and saw the hotel where the reception had taken place. This was the first time she'd been back to this area since her wedding.

Immediately, she felt the searing heat of tears spring to her eyes. Holding them back was virtually impossible. Her chest was burning with the pressure of sorrow and the feeling of loss and her throat felt like sandpaper. The tears were hot against her face as they trailed down her cheeks and dripped off her chin. She didn't even try to hold them back. She gave them no resistance.

She closed her eyes and saw Ryan standing at the foot of the altar waiting for her as she approached the front of the church. His smile had been radiant, his face so happy. Then came the reception, his dance with her and then the traditional dance with his mother. Hank had caught the garter when Ryan had thrown it. This memory brought an image of Hank to the surface. The Hank of old, the warm friendly, loving Hank, not the cold, distant Hank she'd spoken to a couple of nights ago.

"We're here lady" the voice of the cab driver came through Joy's thoughts as she opened her eyes and found herself in the driveway of the Young's estate. The great white columns gracing the front portico still stood as white and regal as she remembered them. The lawns were still impeccably groomed and ablaze with a profusion of color. Charles and Mamie had always liked flowers. Their lawns proved it. There were gardens of flowers, all laid out in intricate designs. To the left of the mansion was a secluded rose garden surrounding delicate white wrought iron chairs and table. To the right was a gigantic old oak tree with a bench built around the trunk. There had been many days when she'd sat there and watched the squirrels jump and play around the yard.

At least the house hasn't changed Joy thought as she climbed out of the cab. She paid the driver and started up the curving drive. Nearing the front door she saw movement inside. At first startled, she soon regained her composure as she remembered Ettie, the Young's housekeeper of many years. Joy rang the doorbell and waited for Ettie to open the door. Not sure if Ettie would recognize her and even remember her, Joy tried desperately to think of something to say when the door opened. Ettie stood there in her immaculate white uniform, older and a little more stooped, with her gray hair pulled back in the unchanging bun.

"Good morning Ettie," Joy started to go on but stopped in mid sentence when Ettie gave a whoop and a wide toothless grin broke the deeply tanned face of the old cajun woman.

"Bon Dieu! Sante Maria! The old woman quickly crossed herself in a sign of the cross. Then just as quickly caught Joy to her bosom and gave her a gigantic hug.

"Mais Chere, come here and let ole Ettie set her eyes on you good. Mais, if you ain't just as pretty as you used to be, I guarantee. Yep, you sure is pretty Miss Joy. Sit down a spell, mon fille, while I catch you a cup of coffee."

Joy gratefully sat and looked around her. She was in the family room surrounded by mementos of Ryan's life. The Youngs had kept all of his pictures and trophies displayed even after all this time had passed. Looking at these, Joy involuntarily shivered as though some premonition was forthcoming. Just then Ettie returned with a tray holding two cups of coffee. This did not dismay Joy as she'd planned on inviting the old woman to sit and talk with her. Joy took her cup and glanced at Ettie. She was slowly lowering her bulk into a chair across from Joy, shaking her head as she did so. Joy noticed the glistening of tears on the old woman's face as she raised it to meet Joy's gaze.

"Ettie, you must know how sorry I am. I arrived here yesterday. Charles passed away shortly after I got to the hospital. He'd aged so much and I had no idea all of this was going on while I was away. I suppose I felt that things couldn't change much more after the accident. I mean, I knew things would change but not this much, this soon. Time just has a way of taking things from you without you realizing it."

Ettie blew her nose and openly crying now, filled Joy in on everything that had happened since her departure from New Orleans. Joy interrupted her now and then to ask a question, but never mentioned Ryan causing Ettie some confusion.

"Chere, did you get to talk to Mr. Charles before he passed on?" Trying to allay some of her confusion, Ettie hesitantly asked Joy.

"Yes Ettie, I did. He struggled so hard to tell me something, but the only thing I could make out was an apology. He seemed desperate to tell me he was sorry. But Ettie, I don't know what he was sorry about. Charles always treated me like a daughter. He had absolutely nothing to apologize to me for."

The old cajun woman stood up and shook her head. She knew what the old man was apologizing for but she surely would not be the one to explain it to Joy.

"Pauvre petite femme, you know Mr. Charles, he had to get right avec le Bon Dieu. I'm sure everything gonna be all right. Just you don't worry, ma petite. Now, is there something I can do for you?"

"No Ettie, thank you. If you don't mind, I'll look around. It's been so long since I've been in this house. I used to love it here when laughter filled these rooms and now they seem so empty." Standing Joy gathered her courage and began her tour of the house, torn between her desire to get in touch with the memories of better times spent there and her curiosity at what she'd find in Charles's desk. She could feel herself pulled in the direction of Ryan's room, but was afraid that she wasn't ready to face that yet.

Curiosity finally won out and she went to Charles's study. She stood in the doorway for a few minutes looking around her. If she closed her eyes she could imagine Charles sitting there behind his huge mahogany desk, trying to look stern but not quite making it because of the persistent twinkle in his eyes. Smiling, Joy remembered the day she and Ryan sat across from Charles in this very room and told him of their plans for marriage after graduation. Charles had leaned back in his high-backed executive chair, then leaned forward trying hard to conceal the approval and affection he held for them and their decision. He'd cleared his throat loudly. Joy and Ryan had looked at each other suppressing the giggles they felt mounting. Charles, not being able to contain his excitement any longer, burst out with a boisterous exclamation of, "that's my son!" Jumping up from his chair he'd come around the desk and grabbed Joy and Ryan in an enormous hug. Just then Mamie, Ryan's mother, had come running into the study to see what was going on. "I've just come in from the French Market and I heard all the commotion. What are ya'll up to now?"

Proudly, he told Mamie the good news. She looked fondly at Ryan and Joy and said she'd been expecting this to happen. She'd congratulated both of them then she'd walked over to Joy, welcoming her to the family as she'd hugged her.

"This calls for a toast," Charles had loudly declared as he brought out a bottle of champagne. They sat drinking their champagne and planning the guest list and the reception.

Joy opened her eyes with a smile on her lips and tears coursing down her cheeks. She walked over to the desk and fondly ran her hands over the surface as in a caress. She opened the main drawer of the desk and there she found the envelope.

It was a business envelope with her name written across the front in Charles's meticulous handwriting. She picked it up with trembling hands. Turning it over, she wondered what was inside. Perhaps she would find out what Charles had apologized for. With tension mounting, she picked up the letter opener and slit the envelope open. Carefully, she pulled a folded piece of paper from the envelope. Unfolding it she found a pair of keys. One was the house key and the other was a car key. The note only contained the name of the law firm that took care of all of Charles's business. No explanations. Only the two keys tagged with Joy's name and the name of the law firm. This is getting stranger by the minute thought Joy, as she folded the note and returned it to the envelope. Picking up the keys she fingered them awhile then tossed them up in the air. She caught them again, and thought, great! Now I won't have to take any more cab rides. But, I'll have to be careful with Charles's Seville. Stupid thoughts, but they were all that surfaced.

Joy looked over to the right hand side of the desk and found Charles's phone index. Checking it she found the name and number of the law firm. She dialed the number and made an appointment for later that day.

Curiosity taken care of, she decided to check out the rest of the house. Hearing Ettie puttering around in the kitchen area, Joy chose to begin in the opposite direction. Little had changed except the color schemes in most of the rooms. The house was a large two story with a gracefully curved staircase in the foyer. Charles and Mamie's bedroom, private bath and dressing room was on the ground floor as well as the living areas, made up of a family room, formal living and dining rooms, kitchen, pantry, two more bathrooms and the sun room that looked out on a perfectly manicured rear lawn and rose garden. Upstairs was Ryan's bedroom and bath, along with a gym Charles and Mamie had set up for his seventeenth birthday. Three other bedrooms were upstairs each with its own bath and sitting room. Three of the upstairs bedrooms faced the front of the property and had french doors opening to a veranda that overlooked the front lawn with its brilliant splashes of color provided by the massive flower gardens. The furnishings in every room were expensive and since Ryan had been an only child, no wear and tear had taken toll on the furniture. It was all still in wonderful shape. Eventually Joy found herself at the door to Ryan's room. As she stepped through the door it seemed that she'd gone back in time, for the room remained virtually unchanged, down to the soft blue carpet and darker blue bedspread and drapes. His trophies lined the shelves on one side of the room. Pictures of her still stood on his bedside table. His New York Yankee baseball cap hung on the pegged rack next to his lettered school jacket. The tapes they had so often listened to, still sat next to the stereo. She passed her hand lovingly over everything she saw. She walked to the closet and found it still filled with his clothes. She walked over to the chest of drawers and found the same there. All of his clothes from underwear to casual walking shorts were still there! Picking up one of his tee shirts, Joy brought it up to her face. She inhaled the fragrance of it. It smelled fresh; recently laundered. "Ryan, I know you are not in this room but darling you feel so close. It's as though I can reach out and hold you," Joy cried into the silent bedroom. She replaced the tee shirt, smoothing it lovingly before she closed the drawer. She stood there a minute and looked around again, allowing her eyes to touch and caress everything in the room. A shiver ran through her causing goose flesh to break out on her arms. She clasped her arms around her body and left the room.

Something is not right here, she thought as she made her way to the kitchen in search of Ettie. She was determined to get some answers. She found Ettie cleaning out the refrigerator. "Ettie, I need to ask you a few questions. Could you spare me a few minutes of your time?"

Ettie turned from her chore as she heard Joy enter the room. "Sure ma petite, go ahead Chere, I'll give you the answer if I can," she replied while wiping her hands on her apron.

"Why are all of Ryan's things just like he left them? And why on earth do his clothes smell fresh after all these years?" Joy jumped right in with her questions, giving no time for pause or preparation.

Ettie hung her head as though guilty of some wrongdoing. "Well, Miss Joy, uh…ya see, Chere…Mr. Charles, he had me leave everything just like they be the day the accident happened." Shrugging, she added, "and I just do what he told me. Kind of spooks me when I go in there though. I sure can tell you dat. Yessiree Bob, it sure do spook me. Yep." Joy reached over and patted Ettie on the back while thanking her. She still wasn't sure what was going on, but as soon as she found out information from the attorney, changes would be made. She would make sure of that.

Walking back into the study, thoughts of her later appointment came to mind. She supposed the attorney would tell her that she would inherit something. No matter what, she was Ryan's wife and that alone entitled her to do what she wanted with his things. A little voice in the back of her mind told her to take care of them now. Charles was gone and she had the time to do it. But she adamantly pushed the tiny voice away. Face it Joy, she told herself, you can't do anything with his things. You're not ready yet. Suddenly she had a feeling of what things must have been like for Charles and Mamie, and she understood a little better why things were the way they were.

Looking at her watch, Joy thought of lunch and Shaze. Thinking this was a good time to call him, she dialed the hotel and asked for his room.

He answered after a few short rings. "Where are you Joy?" he demanded, "You've been gone all morning and I was beginning to worry."

"I told you this morning that I had to come to Charles's house. It looks like I'll have a lot of business to tend to and it may take awhile. You wouldn't believe what I've found over here."

"What did you find? A mystery man?" Shaze sounded sarcastic.

"No, no mystery man, but I may have discovered a mystery. Would you believe it if I told you that Ryan's room was left exactly the way it was before the accident?"

"That doesn't surprise me. It seems something the old man would do."

"What do you mean, Shaze? You sound like you knew Charles. Did you?"

"Uh, don't be silly Joy, how would I know Charles? I'm just assuming that would be something he would do to keep the memory of Ryan alive. After all, you did tell me that Ryan was this old man's only child. Maybe after Ryan's death the old man became crazy or something. That's all I meant." His voice took on a defensive tone.

"Okay, I'm sorry I jumped on you like that. I guess my nerves are about shot. Anyway, going into Ryan's room made me feel weird, almost like he was with me or something. It felt strange. Not in a scary kind of way, just weird." Her voice trailed off giving Shaze the feeling she was speaking more to herself than to him. Getting back to the reason for her call she continued, "how about coming to meet me for lunch? I have an appointment with the attorney later this afternoon, but we could see each other for a little while."

Shaze jumped on the unexpected invitation, "that's the best thing I've heard since I got here. I'll grab my jacket and be there shortly. And Joy…"

"Yes?"

"I'm sorry for last night. I don't know what got into me. You do know that I love you, don't you?"

"Yes, Shaze and I love you too."

"I'll see you in a little bit. Bye love."

As Joy replaced the receiver she realized she hadn't given him the address. Immediately she dialed the hotel again, however, this time she didn't get an answer. Oh well, she thought, I suppose he'll realize he doesn't have the address and will call me from God knows where. Again, she thought of Shaze's strange behavior since their arrival in New Orleans. Shrugging her shoulders, she walked into the kitchen to ask Ettie about lunch.

Within the hour, Joy heard the doorbell ring. Sensing it was Shaze, she realized how badly she missed him; a familiar face from her new world. Opening the door, she threw her arms around him, "Oh, Shaze it is good to see you." Shaze returned her hug a little stiffly and a dark scowl showed on his face. He'd forgotten how impressive this damn house was. Comparing the luxury of this place to the poverty he was brought up in had turned his mood sour.

Puzzled, Joy looked into his face. Not wanting to initiate another argument she ignored his mood. The memory of last night's conflict was bad enough.

Disappointed in his mood she tried to dispel it. "Man, I must look like hell," she teased hoping to loosen him up. Shaze looked into her face, "If this is what I can find in hell, open the damn doors, I'm coming in," he growled as he pulled her to him.

"You crazy man! C'mon, let's get some lunch. I can use some of your wit and charm." They linked arms and set off for the kitchen. Nearing the kitchen Ettie's lunch preparations could be heard but Joy's chatter drowned out the sounds so it was with surprise that Shaze met up with Ettie as he walked through the kitchen doors. Before Joy could make introductions, Shaze spun around and bolted for the front doors. Mystified by Shaze's behavior, Joy mumbled an apology to Ettie and followed him outside.

"Hey, wait up. Wait up a minute. Shaze, where do you think you're going? What in the hell happened in there?"

He turned and answered her with an icy stare, "I thought you were by yourself. Why didn't you tell me someone was here with you?"

Taken aback by the harshness of his voice Joy stuttered, "It's only Ettie. She's been with this family for as long as I can remember."

"I don't care who in hell she is, or how long she's been in this damned family. I didn't expect anyone to be here. She surprised me, and you know damn good and well that I don't like surprises."

"Well, she's here and she's going to stay," Joy shot back. Realizing the tone of her voice, she finished the statement in a softer tone, "for now anyway." She was quickly forgetting her vow to hold her temper in check and was becoming increasingly agitated by his reaction to seeing Ettie and his whole attitude toward this trip.

The side of Shaze that Beth had warned her about, and that Joy always denied existed, was rearing its ugly head. She was beginning to see the side of Shaze that Beth had seen. Beth had tried to warn her about him. She had always told Joy there was something about Shaze that rubbed her the wrong way. Thinking perhaps Beth was a little jealous, she had brushed off all warnings. Now she was starting to wonder if Beth was right.

"Look, I'll see you back at the hotel, that is if you decide to come back," Shaze shouted over his shoulder as he began to walk away toward the driveway.

"Shaze, Shaze wait! Come back. Please don't go. Tell me what's wrong. What did I do to upset you?" Joy was running down the drive imploring him not to go. "What's gotten into you? You've been acting strangely since we've gotten here. Are you frightened of something? Talk to me dammit!"

Joy's words shot through Shaze bringing him back into focus. What was he thinking of, running like a thief in the night? His head snapped up as he came to an abrupt stop. Turning, he hissed at Joy, "Scared? What do you mean asking what I'm scared of?" Grabbing her arm roughly, he spat at her through clenched teeth, "Nothing in this damned place scares me, do you hear me?"

"But...but, Shaze, you've been acting weird, not at all like yourself and I'm concerned. That's all. That's all I meant by it," Joy cried.

"Tell me! Just tell me, damn it! What do you find so frigging weird about my behavior? What is causing you concern?" Shaze was furious. More at himself than with Joy but he wouldn't let on to that with her. Let her believe he was angry with her. Maybe that would distract her from dwelling on his erratic behavior.

They stood there in Charles's front yard, under the big oak tree lashing out at each other. Joy at first, tried not to anger him more than he already was, then said the hell with it, and told him the reasons for her concern. "First of all, you didn't even want to come with me. That's pretty damn strange for someone who has become my shadow, never letting me out of his sight for fear of God knows what. Then your obsession with "the old man" as you so tactlessly put it, so eager to find out if he'd died or not, like it mattered to you. Now, to top it all off, your reaction to Ettie. The poor woman was just in the kitchen preparing lunch for us. I know you must've scared the hell out of her. Your behavior was just plain rude, there's no other way to put it." Touching his arm she softened her voice and cried, "Shaze, I've never seen you act like this before and it worries me. You don't seem to be the same man I fell in love with and agreed to marry. What caused the change? Do you know someone here? Is there a reason why you shouldn't be here?"

Joy had come very close to secrets Shaze carried deep inside himself. Seeing the tears in her eyes and hearing the tenderness in her voice, he softened his tone and relaxed as much as he could. Taking her in his arms, he apologized. "Joy, I'm sorry. Babe, I've been such a jerk. Can you forgive me? You're right, you know. I am scared."

"You're scared? My God, of what?" Joy could see tears glistening in his eyes and this threw her. What could bring this man to the brink of tears? He'd always been so cool, so masculine in his manner and this just wasn't in his character.

"I'm scared of what the attorney will tell you. Maybe Charles has left you everything. Joy, you will be a wealthy woman and maybe you won't need me anymore. I'm scared of losing you. That fear has me upset."

"Oh, my darling. You must never be afraid of losing me. Shaze, no matter what the attorney tells me, I'll still love you and I still plan to marry you. Nothing can change that."

Shaze looked at Joy. Her large, brown, trust filled eyes returned his gaze. Hugging her to him he prayed that what she had just said was true. Part of him loved her and needed her love and the other part of him wanted only what she could give him, and love had nothing to do with it. Shaze felt torn between the two desires. This is getting tough. I almost blew it this time. Next time I might not be so lucky.

The thoughts whirled around his head. "Maybe I should leave." The words sprang out of his mouth, surprising him. Joy looked startled.

"Leave? What do you mean? Leave here or leave New Orleans?"

Yeah, that's it, he thought. That's my way out before I screw things up royally. Thoughts were now coming fast and furious. That seemed like the perfect plan, although it meant having to wait for news from Joy. But, since he seemed to be having such a rough time keeping it together, it might be better if he left.

"I've been thinking, love. You have a lot on your mind and may have a lot of business to take care of and you sure don't need me and my insecurities to burden you. So maybe it would be better for both of us, if I went back to Los Angeles and checked on the store."

"I guess you're right," the words came a little hesitantly while she sat there a couple of minutes mulling over his suggestion. "Yeah, I suppose that would be the best thing to do. But Shaze…"

"Yes, Joy?"

"Look, let's give this thing a little more time. I know this afternoon will be rough and I feel that I will need you. I know I haven't spent much time with you since our arrival, but knowing that you are in the same city and nearby is such a comfort."

"You know I'll do anything for you babe, and I really do think I ought to go back, but if you really want me to stay awhile longer, consider it done." Good, he thought, maybe he'd be able to find out something about the inheritance before he left. The sooner he found out, the sooner his other plans could go into effect.

Joy looked up at the tall, tanned man in front of her, grateful for his consideration but at the same time perplexed at his complexity. Feeling she really did have enough to contend with, without having to worry herself with his crazy moods and fears, she pushed thoughts of his behavior aside. Looking at her watch she said, "Well, we stood here arguing our lunch time away. I'm sorry Shaze, but I need to get ready to see the attorney. I'll meet you back at the hotel."

"Yeah, I'm not so hungry anyway." Leaning down, he kissed Joy lightly on the lips and started down the driveway.

She watched him walk away, with a smart little swagger to his walk. His strut was one belonging to someone who had not a care in the world. His mood had switched again. Joy shook her head then called out, "hey, you've forgotten the car. Don't you want to take it?"

"No, I want to ride the trolleys. It's been years since I've…"

She stood at the curb waving goodbye and wondering about what was to come as she watched him walk out of sight.

# CHAPTER 5

Joy freshened her makeup, got into Charles's Cadillac Seville, and drove to the attorney's. She was punctual, as usual, and was soon met by Mr. LaBauve, the attorney in charge of Charles's affairs. Although portly, he exuded an air of conviction and dignity. Grasping his hand in a firm shake Joy confirmed her quick assessment of his character. There was no doubt in her mind why Charles had chosen this person to handle his affairs. She introduced herself to him and sat down.

"Mrs. Young, I'm so sorry to hear about your father-in-law. His death will be deeply mourned by all who knew him. He was a good man. Yes, a good man indeed." Mr. LaBauve removed his eyeglasses and looked at Joy with kindness.

"Thank you for your sympathy Mr. LaBauve. You know, I hadn't seen Charles or his wife in several years and I was shocked, to say the least, to hear that he was asking for me. I suppose this trip is full of surprises. I've found out that Mamie has passed on also. I'm almost afraid to see what happens next." Joy gave the attorney a direct look.

The attorney returned her look as he asked her, "Mrs. Young, did you get to talk to Charles before he passed on?"

"Not for very long. He seemed desperate to tell me something but the poor darling was having such a hard time breathing, I'm sorry to say that the only thing I could make out was an apology. I can't figure out why he felt he needed to apologize to me. He and Mamie always treated me with kindness and affection. This really puzzles me. Can you perhaps shed light on this apology? Do you know what Charles was trying to tell me?" Joy looked imploringly at the lawyer. He stood up and opened a file folder that had been on his desk.

"Uh hum…Mrs. Young," he cleared his throat before going on, "I'm holding Charles's will. Your father-in-law was not only a kind man, Mrs. Young, but he was a generous one as well."

"Charles's will? What does that have to do with me? Has he named me in his will?" Then as an afterthought she added, "Oh, yes I suppose he would, since I had been married to his only son. Forgive me, Mr. LaBauve, I'm not thinking too clearly. So much has happened since my arrival yesterday. It's hard to grasp everything."

"I understand and please don't apologize. You are named in the will. In fact, you, Mrs. Young, are the sole beneficiary of Charles's vast holdings."

"The sole beneficiary? You can't mean that Charles has left everything to me!"

"Yes ma'am, that's precisely what I'm telling you. Charles has left everything, which includes all his stores, all stocks and bonds, the real estate holdings including rentals, summer home and the house on St. Charles Avenue. The list goes on Mrs. Young, shall I continue?"

Overwhelmed by what she was hearing Joy shook her head from side to side. "Thank you, but I'm sure I can find out more about it later. You've given me enough to think about for right now." Shaking her head in astonishment she almost missed the attorney's next words.

"Mrs. Young, like I said before everything is yours except one special account. That account can only be used as needed for the expenses incurred in the care of Charles's son."

Joy's head snapped up and the attorney had her full attention. With eyes grown large at the word son she gasped, "his what?"

Slowly the portly little man raised his head and looked Joy directly in the eyes. "His son. Ryan."

"Ryan? Is this some kind of sick joke?" Angry now and bewildered, Joy stood up. "I'm utterly amazed that a person with your reputation could do this to me. To any person who has lost a loved one. What kind of game are you playing, Mr. LaBauve? Tell me, are you enjoying this, because I'm not and I don't have to stay here and listen to this nonsense. I was married to Ryan and Ryan is dead. DEAD. Do you hear me Mr. LaBauve? He was killed in a car accident on our wedding day." Joy struggled to hold back threatening tears. "I find this cruel and uncalled for and I, uh, I feel that an apology is called for." With nothing more to say, Joy angrily walked to the door.

"Wait, Mrs. Young. Please hear me out. I'm sorry. I wasn't aware you were under the assumption that your husband had been killed."

"Assumption? I know, Mr. LaBauve, that my husband was killed that night. Both his father and mother told me once I regained consciousness. They said, 'We're sorry, but Ryan did not survive the explosion.' I heard them, Mr. LaBauve. Now, seven years later, you're telling me he is alive and I'm supposed to believe you."

The attorney's heart was breaking for this poor little creature that was trying with all her might to hold on to her sanity. He hated dealings like this and had never imagined Charles to conduct business like this. Reaching into Charles's folder he pulled out a letter addressed to Joy. He hadn't questioned anything when Charles had given it to him. He'd just taken it and placed it in the folder with the rest of Charles's important papers, thinking that it was just a good bye letter. But, now he understood. It was more than a good bye letter. He was willing to bet that it was a letter of explanation and that was the reason behind the apology.

Keeping his presumption to himself he placed a gentle hand on Joy's shoulder.

"Perhaps this will answer some of your questions, honey. I'm so sorry to be the one to break this news to you. Now, I'll leave you alone for a few minutes. If you need me, just call out and I'll be here in a flash. Okay?"

Joy glared back at him, defiance shooting from her eyes. "Mr. LaBauve, if what you've said to me is true and if this offers some degree of explanation, then I must apologize to you. It's hard to believe anyone as kind as Charles would set out to hurt me like this. I find it very hard to believe that anyone would be so cold hearted as to keep two people who love each other the way Ryan and I did apart for seven years."

Still dazed by everything she'd been told, she reached out and took hold of the letter. With trembling fingers and racing heart she slowly opened the letter. It was written in Charles's meticulous hand-writing

> Our Dearest Joy, it began,
>
> By now you must know that Ryan is alive. Please, don't judge us too harshly for what we've done.
> While you were comatose we were told of Ryan's condition. The prognosis was anything but good. The doctors have confirmed that seventy percent of Ryan's body is covered in third degree burns. These burns have been responsible for other conditions affecting his recovery. Scar tissue from the burns has disfigured him almost beyond recognition and has cost him the use of one eye. He is paralyzed from the waist down. I suppose some would say that he is alive, but we say that he exists and nothing more.
> You were so young and beautiful and life had already dealt you an unfair hand. We felt that you still had your whole life ahead of you, while Ryan's was for all intent and purpose, finished. We knew that the heartbreak you went through at the news of his death would be nothing compared to the agony you would suffer having to see him the way he is now. We told Ryan that you moved away and we felt in our hearts

that he was relieved that you would be spared his suffering. Time has gone by now and our health is failing, so we decided to write this to you in hopes that we could somehow justify our decision and our actions. Hopefully, someday you will understand why we did what we did and perhaps you will find forgiveness in your heart for us. I'm sure, right now as you're reading this, you're feeling angry with us, but I sincerely pray that the day will come when you will be able to agree with our decision. Joy, we hope you will come to realize that our actions were done out of love for you. We're sorry that you and Ryan were robbed of the love and life together that you were entitled to.

Our attorney will tell you the rest, but we needed to tell you this ourselves.

Your loving In-Laws,

Charles and Mamie Young

Joy could not see for the tears streaming from her eyes. Ryan was alive! Barely alive, by what she had just read, but alive. Something in the deep recesses of her psyche had prevented her from totally believing in Ryan's death, although reason and reality had told her otherwise. No it can't be, she told herself, but deep down inside her soul, she felt a confirmation. She read again, the first line of the now tear splattered letter and felt her heart tremble with joy. Was it only joy, or was there a little trepidation mixed in with it?

Joy looked up. Mr. LaBauve was standing in front of her. "Oh, I didn't hear you come in," Joy squeaked out as she reached for the tissue he was extending to her. Still stunned by what she'd read she stuttered, "Wh…Wh…what does this mean? I can't believe that Ryan is still living. They told me he was dead. They had no right to do this. He needs me. He must have needed me all this time."

My God, I was planning on getting married in a few days. If Charles had not died, I would never have known that Ryan, my husband, was living. Joy's face displayed an array of emotions as she weighed this information. First disbelief, then anger and finally sorrow. Her sobs were intense as she sat there.

LaBauve stood there silently while she gave herself up to the ravaging tears. When they seemed to subside he handed her a glass of water and continued with the information in the will, offering at last any assistance she might need now and in the future.

"There's one question Mr. LaBauve, before I leave."

"Yes, and what might that be?"

"Could you please tell me where Ryan is?"

"I'm not sure, to be honest with you. There was someone, a friend of Ryan's, I believe, that Charles spoke of highly. It seems that this friend has kept in touch with Ryan. Perhaps he can help you. I'm sorry, Mrs. Young that I can't help you with more information. In his affairs concerning Ryan, Charles chose to be somewhat guarded."

"I'm sorry too, Mr. LaBauve, and you have already been a great help to me." Standing she extended her hand to the attorney that had just told her she was now an extremely wealthy woman and that she was indeed not a widow as she had presumed for the past seven years. "Thank you and I'm sure I will be in touch." Stunned, the petite, dark haired beauty walked out of the office.

Back at the hotel with the numbness wearing off, Joy kicked off her shoes and let her aching body fall onto the bed. Staring up at the ceiling she mentally went over her conversation with LaBauve. He had mentioned a name. No, her mind argued, he didn't mention a name. He said that a friend had kept in touch. A friend? That friend could only be Hank. Although Ryan was well liked and had many friends, the only ones that could have stood by him through all of this were herself and Hank. Hank! More pieces fell into place. Grabbing the phone directory she quickly turned the pages until she found the Morgans. Skimming the names with her fingers she found the listing. Hank Morgan 555-0001. Recalling the arrogance Hank treated her with a couple of days earlier, Joy hesitated but not for long. "I'll call him," she said aloud in the empty room as excitement built up in her. "He may not want to speak to me, but it's time his attitude changes." Waiting for the connection to be made, the thought occurred to her that perhaps Hank wouldn't help her. After all he had sounded quite upset with her over the phone. Before she could lose her courage and hang up, she heard the annoying dull beep of a busy line. Damn! Joy was torn between disappointment at the delay in finding Ryan and relief at not having to speak to someone who obviously hated her. Disappointment won as she replaced the receiver into its holder.

Lying back in bed she decided to plan what she would do next, but before any plans came to mind, the thought of Shaze torpedoed her mind. Damn! What am I going to tell Shaze? No telling how he would take this news, especially when she'd told him just a couple of hours ago that he was in no danger of losing her and that she was still planning to marry him. Now, that was impossible. Marriage to Shaze was definitely out of the question.

Confused, she thought of her feelings for Shaze. She loved him, but she had never stopped loving Ryan, even when she had thought he was dead. Now that she knew he was still living, she could feel a resurgence of love for him.

I need to talk to Shaze, but not right now. I'll do it later. I can't think of him right now, she argued with herself. Shoving aside thoughts of Shaze, she instead allowed the excitement at the prospect of seeing Ryan again, to fill her mind

All she wanted to think of was the fact that Ryan was alive. She wanted to shout it from the rooftops, no matter what his condition was. She had promised at her wedding to love him through bad times as well as good times and in sickness and in health and she meant to stand by her promise. To make things even better, Hank was still around. That eased Joy's mind a great deal.

During a leisurely soak a few minutes later her thoughts again became obscured with worry and doubt. Would Ryan recognize her?

Would he even want to see her? Suppose Ryan refused to see her, after all it had been a very long time. Maybe he'd stopped loving her. What if he thought she'd deserted him? If these thoughts were indeed true, she would not be able to blame him.

A surge of anger directed toward her in laws arose in her like bile coming to the surface. She tried to put herself in their place to see if she could understand what would have driven them to make the decisions they'd made regarding her and Ryan's future. As hard as she tried, she just couldn't understand what possessed them. She knew the decisions had been made without malice. They loved her, this she truly believed. Charles's leaving everything to her proved that. Or did it? Perhaps it was a way of assuaging their guilt for the terrible mistake they'd made when they played God with her and Ryan's lives.

Well, she thought, what's done is done. I can't go back and I can't change things, so I'll just start over as of this minute. It sounded like a good resolution to begin with. Joy closed her eyes and allowed the hot water to soothe away her anger and fear of the future.

The ringing telephone jarred Joy out of her relaxed state in the tub. Clambering out of the tub she wrapped a towel around her and ran into the bedroom to answer the phone.

"Hello, beautiful, it's your adoring love slave at your service." "Shaze! She wasn't ready for this yet, but he did sound much better than he had earlier that afternoon.

"Shaze! She was just thinking of calling you," she lied.

"You were? Well love, I just couldn't wait any longer. I needed to hear your voice. How did your meeting go?"

"My meeting...uh, well I guess you could say that it went well. I had quite a few surprises waiting for me."

Detecting an underlying excitement in Joy's voice he said "from the sound of your voice, I would say the surprises were good."

Shaze had picked up on the excitement in Joy's voice, but little did he know that the inheritance was not responsible for the happiness he detected.

"The surprises were very good. It seems Charles left me all of his holdings." She told him what she knew he wanted to hear.

"All of his holdings? Just what does that mean?"

"That means exactly what it sounds like. He's left everything that he owned to me. I was named his sole beneficiary." Joy became agitated at his feigned ignorance of what she was telling him.

Shaze exuded a low whistle. "That must mean, m'love, that you are now a very wealthy woman. I suppose one could now call you a woman of means."

Joy perceived the excitement in his voice but she had no way of knowing that the excitement was for himself, not for her.

"Let's go out and celebrate, Joy m'love." Shaze was ready to celebrate; he had waited a long time for this.

Joy declined saying that the day had been rough for her and she felt she needed to get some rest. What she didn't tell him was that she wanted to be left alone with her thoughts of Ryan tonight. His face was the last one she wanted to see before sleep overcame her and she didn't mind that it would be only in her imagination.

Shaze reluctantly bade her good night and ended the conversation.

Tomorrow, Joy thought as she dozed off to sleep. Tomorrow I'll tell Shaze that I've changed my mind about his staying here. I'll tell him I reconsidered his offer to check on the store and I'll stay here to tie things up. Then tomorrow I'll get in touch with Hank and maybe I'll get to see my dear, sweet Ryan. She closed her eyes and for once her dreams of Ryan were not interrupted.

The next day dawned sunny and warm. Joy awakened feeling refreshed and like a new woman. She felt like she had been given a new lease on life. Smiling, she went through her daily routine of getting dressed, and then went to Shaze's room. He greeted her at the door with a smile that once had the power to make her warm all over. Now, it filled her with dread because there was no way she could marry him. Not now that Ryan was alive.

Taking her in his arms he hugged her tightly to him, reveling in the delicate scent of her. She always reminded him of moonlight and orchids. Today was no different. She was dressed for the Louisiana humidity, in a white cotton sundress with small lavender flowers printed at random on the dress. She completed her ensemble with white and lavender sandals and a large white straw hat with lavender ribbon around the crown. Pushing her an arm's length away from himself, he gave an appreciative whistle. "Am I just imagining it, or are you a changed woman? They say that money talks and little lady, you just proved that. You look like a million dollars already and I know you don't have it yet. I would feel the same if I were in your shoes. Man, if I would have received the news you did yesterday, I would be flying high" Shaze just seemed to rattle on and Joy didn't stop him.

I am flying high, she thought, but surely not because of the money. Changing the subject Joy asked him "how about coming to breakfast with a hungry woman?"

"Hungry for what?"

Joy could see a lecherous glint in his eyes. The one thing that she and Shaze argued over was sex. She had to be the only twenty-five year old virgin this side of the Mississippi.

Shaze had tried to change that status, but she somehow managed to hold him off. They had come close a few times, when she allowed her body to give in to the desires stirred in her. She always managed to prevent anything happening. On the brink of tasting what she never had, her feelings would take an abrupt turn and stop. Cold. This had often led to an argument between a frustrated Shaze and an even more frustrated Joy. She always reasoned it out as the result of her strict moral beliefs. She knew now it was because of her love and devotion to Ryan.

Playfully slapping at his hands, she pushed him to the door telling him she was hungry for food and nothing else. He joked back saying the only thing that was changed in her was her financial status, that she was still the hardest conquest he'd met as of yet.

Joy didn't say anything in reply but was thinking, I'm not a conquest yet, dear Shaze. You have not conquered anything.

As they closed the hotel door Joy heard Shaze whistling some tune about wanting to be rich and being in the money now.

Joy emitted a big sigh of relief as she dropped Shaze off at the airport. She was surprised at his ready acceptance of her request that he return to L.A. Now she was free to get in touch with Hank. With luck, she would get to see Ryan. A shiver of anticipation ran through her. She began whistling a tune with the radio as she drove back to the hotel.

Once at the hotel, she threw her handbag down and picked up the phone. Please be home, she prayed, as she dialed Hank's number. She didn't stop to think what reaction Hank would have when he heard her voice. She just assumed that of course he would change, once he realized she had held her word and had returned to New Orleans, and things would just be like they used to be. She'd convinced herself that the thoughts and fears of the previous night, of him hating her were absurd.

In what seemed to Joy to be hours, but in reality was just a few beats of time, the phone was answered. With heart racing, Joy realized it was an answering machine, stating that Hank was not home, the caller could leave a message or if it was an emergency, they could reach him at his place of employment, Morgan's Oil Exploration & Survey. Joy hung up the phone without leaving a message. Deciding that it would be better if she went to see Hank instead of leaving a message, she found the listing for Morgan's Oil Exploration & Survey and dialed the number. Once the connection was made Joy asked for directions to get there, thanked the girl and hung up. Picking up her handbag she left in search of Hank.

Joy found the address easily and was very impressed at what she found. Hank, it seemed, was doing fine for himself. The office was housed in a multi-storied glass building in the business district of New Orleans. Consulting the directory in the lobby she found that Hank's office was on the eighth floor. Her state of excitement was such that she was beyond actually thinking. Her actions were almost automated, with not much thought behind them. Her main goal at this stage was to find Ryan. The elevator doors opened to an outer office carpeted in deep blue with potted plants and trees dominating the decor. In fact, everything down to the smartly dressed reception-ist smelled of success and was done in good taste. Joy was greeted with a smile and asked if she had an appointment with Mr. Morgan. Returning the receptionist's smile, Joy shook her head no but asked her please, if possible, to tell Mr. Morgan that she wanted to see him.

"Your name please?" the receptionist reached for the phone.

"Joy Young," she replied. "Mrs. Joy Young." She tried to read the receptionist's expression as she repeated Joy's name to Hank, but professionalism ran high in this employee. Her face remained impas-sive, no expression change at all. Now that Joy was actually here, some of her feelings of anxiety were resurfacing. She watched ner-vously as the woman behind the desk hung the phone up. She informed Joy that Mr. Morgan was on a long distance phone call but that his secretary would tell him that she was here and waiting. Real-ity set in and she realized that Hank's business was larger than she first thought it to be and that he was now an important man. Maybe she should have called and made an appointment. Suppose he was too busy to see her? Worry and fear were running through her mind as she sat waiting for Hank. She picked up a magazine and began thumbing through the pages not paying attention to what she saw.

In a few minutes she heard an inner door open and heard a slightly familiar voice then another door opened and Hank stood before her. Joy looked up at the sound of the first door opening and thus was face to face with Hank as he walked through the second door.

# CHAPTER 6

*J*oy stood and took the extended hand Hank offered her. His voice, filled with incredulity at the aspect of seeing her in his office, gave her a warm feeling as nostalgia swept over her. The warmth soon vanished, however, for when she lifted her eyes to look into his, she was met with cold steel. The friendliness she'd heard in his voice, as he'd greeted her, was betrayed by the emotion she saw in his eyes. She hadn't expected jubilation but she certainly had expected some degree of warmth coming from him. Instead of warmth, his steady gray gaze was hard and cold and held a degree of distance in it. It was overall a look she was not expecting and definitely one she did not understand. He looked at her as one would look at a stranger.

"Damn, you'd think I was his enemy instead of one of his oldest friends. Well, time has a way of changing things," she told herself. She tried to reassure herself that Hank's feelings toward her weren't important. What mattered now, was the task at hand and that was finding Ryan. But his coldness nagged at her as he escorted her to his office.

"Alex, this is Joy Young, an acquaintance from the past. Joy, this is Alex, my personal secretary."

Joy smiled at the svelte blonde Hank had just introduced her to, only to be met with a cold stare and an equally cold smile.

"Alex, hold all calls please. I don't want to be disturbed." Hank exchanged a warm smile with his secretary as he walked behind Joy into his office.

The exchange of warmth was not lost on Joy. She was willing to bet that Hank and his personal secretary were romantically involved and the woman was a mite jealous. That accounted for the coldness she sensed in Alex, but why the coldness in Hank? Ah, well, his coldness toward her was his problem, she decided. I'm here for one purpose and one purpose only. And that is to get to Ryan. To hell with them if they have a problem with me, she thought.

Once in the office, silence hung between them like a huge wall. They took advantage of the silence and quickly assessed each other. Allowing her gaze to sweep over Hank as he propped himself up against the window ledge, Joy quickly concluded that he had surely improved with age, although he never really needed much improvement. His dark hair was still dark with just slight touches of gray at the temple and his blue-gray eyes were now more gray than blue. He had added a moustache and beard, but kept these impeccably groomed. He was slightly taller than average and by no means could be considered tall. His physique was well tended and although lean, quite muscular. She remembered him being a handsome teenager but her memories of him could not compare with the handsome man that stood across the room from her. "Uhmm, no wonder Alex was jealous," she thought. Then the idea of Alex being jealous of her brought a hint of a smile to the corners of her mouth, as she took a seat.

Looking around her, she had the feeling she'd just stepped out of the vacuum her life had been lived in, and into the real world. Life had gone on despite her leaving. Not that she'd expected everything to fall apart, but she had stopped living. Since the accident, she had existed, not lived. All in a matter of minutes this revelation made itself known to her.

Joy was not the only one lost in thought. Hank also took advantage of the silence to drink in the sight he often longed to see. Joy! The name was so appropriate, for every time he so much as thought of her that was the sentiment he felt. Even lately, when he tried desperately to hate her for running out on Ryan, he didn't succeed. He could remember the first time he had set eyes on her in high school. She'd walked right into Ryan and him and his heart was immediately hers. She stole the hearts of every male in every class she walked into that day and as luck would have it, the one she claimed belonged to his best friend.

He'd tried to date other girls, but none could make him feel the way Joy could. So he'd hung around Ryan and Joy and they had become the "trio". Every time she'd looked at Ryan, he would imagine it was him she was looking at. He had treasured the vision of her walking down the aisle on her wedding day and had taken it into the Army with him. He could still remember the tears he'd shed during his flight to basic training. She had looked so perfect.

Ryan knew about his feelings for Joy. He had always known. Often, when they spoke about her in those high school years, Ryan had promised to love her for both of them. Hank looked at her now and a surge of love rushed forward. He noticed how her hairstyle had changed and the light in her eyes had dimmed. He wondered why her hair was now worn loose and covering the left side of her face. She had always worn her hair pulled back in a barrette. He'd always liked how little curls had always escaped the confines of the barrette and framed her face, accentuating her soft brown eyes.

"The beard and moustache…"

"The new hair style is very…"

They both began to talk at the same time, and then both apologized at the same time. Hank being the gentleman he was, gave her the opportunity to talk first.

"Well Hank, it seems that time has treated you well. I'm impressed by all of this," she gave a graceful sweep of her hand, indicating the rich pecan paneling and tasteful furnishings surrounding them. "Who would've guessed seven years ago that today you would be a successful businessman?"

"Yes, well what can I say? Life is full of surprises, isn't it Joy? What have you done in these past seven years?"

"After the accident, I moved to Los Angeles and opened the jewelry store that Charles and Mamie gave to me, uh, to us."

At this slight implication of Ryan, Hank felt himself stiffen. His loyalty to Ryan surfaced and Joy felt the difference in him. "Damn, what's with this guy," Joy mused.

Clearing her throat she decided to stop beating around the bush, since it now seemed the old way of life and the bond of the "trio" was annulled. "Hank, I know you're a busy man and consequently I do not wish to take up much of your time. I'm here because I understand you have kept in touch with Ryan over the years and I would like to see him."

"You what?" Hank jumped to his feet. His eyes were blazing and Joy could see the veins in his neck stand out. "After all this time, you decide to just walk into our lives, like you did in high school, and demand to see someone you walked out on at a time that he needed you most? You've got to be crazy, woman. I knew when Charles asked me to call you something like this was going to happen. I'll tell you right now, Joy, I don't want any part of this. Do you hear me? I won't be responsible for any more pain being inflicted on Ryan."

Hank was angry and Joy didn't really understand why, but her nerves were strung out to the max and she reacted to his reaction.

"Oh, get over it Hank. I don't know what crawled into your morning cereal to ruin your day, but I do know that I don't deserve to be spoken to in this manner. How dare you! How dare you talk to me this way? For your information, I'm here because Charles requested that I come to New Orleans remember? I got here before he died and I'm here because of him. I didn't ask for any of this crap. I was perfectly happy where I was. My whole damned life is turned upside down, and now I have to sit here and take rudeness from you. Well, buddy, take your information and shove it, you hear me. I'll find Ryan on my own." Joy's eyes were shooting sparks as she stood in front of Hank with hands balled into fists.

If Joy could have seen herself, she would have been proud of the way she was standing up to this antagonist; for that was how she now saw Hank. He was her adversary. Once a friend, now an enemy, someone whose sole purpose was to antagonize her at every turn. Well, I can do without him, she thought.

Hank sat back in his chair sputtering, "Charles? What did you say about Charles dying? When did this happen? I knew his time was near but I assumed I'd be notified when it actually happened. I wanted to be there with him."

Joy, still angry, walked to the door of the office, yanked it open and with eyes still sparking she spat out, "Charles died last night." Let Hank think that she had walked out on Ryan; she was so upset with him that she didn't think he should know that she'd just found out that he was living. As she started to walk out of the door, Hank jumped up from behind his desk and in two strides was beside her.

Grabbing her arm he hissed, "Wait! Joy, you can't tell me this and then just walk out. What time did he pass on?" He was killing time; the need to keep her there awhile longer was burning within him. He needed to keep her from walking out of his life like she'd walked out of Ryan's. His mind told him she was trouble and he needed to rid himself of her but his heart told him differently. Now that she was back, maybe he'd have a chance to win her heart. This thought quickened his pulse but the old sense of loyalty to Ryan made him feel like a heel.

Spinning around, Joy jerked her arm away from him. Hank held his hands up in the air, in way of apology and asked her to please close the door and sit back down. Reluctantly, she closed the door but refused his offer of a seat. She would answer his questions if he had any and would listen to what he would say but that was it. She decided she didn't need his assistance whatsoever. She would do what she had to and she would do it by herself.

Hank began asking her about Charles. She told him how she'd called Dr. Peters the night Hank called her about Charles's request then an hour later she was on her way to New Orleans. She had arrived just before Charles passed away. She told him she didn't know how long she would be here in New Orleans but that she had some business to attend to and that was her only plans for now.

Hank meanwhile was thinking, aha, Charles is dead and Ryan must've inherited everything and that was her reason for trying to find him. He had to think nasty things about her, although in the deepest recesses of his heart and mind, he knew them to be untrue.

"Joy, I'm truly sorry to hear about Charles. And about Ryan, Joy, I would ask you to stay away for awhile."

"Stay away for awhile? Don't you think I've stayed away long enough?" Joy shot back at him.

"It doesn't matter what I think," the iciness in his voice chilled the room, "all that I'm concerned about is Ryan and how he will take the news of his father's death. I really don't think he could take the shock of seeing you after all this time and the news of his father's death all at once. All I'm asking you to do is wait a week or two and let him adjust to the news of Charles's death first, then if you still want to see him, I'll bring you to him."

Taken aback by Hank's concern for Ryan and her lack of it, Joy hung her head and felt the tears sting the back of her eyelids. She looked at Hank with her incredibly soft eyes swimming in tears and stretched out her hand while thanking him. It was all she could do to keep from screaming out at the injustice of having to wait some more.

Hank reached out and felt his heart jump as he took her hand in his. He looked down at her and forcing himself to sound hard, told her that he would get in touch with her in a few days. She left him the number of the hotel and walked out of the room, out of the building and Hank hoped not out of his life.

The next week flew by quickly for Joy though she cried herself to sleep every night after waiting in vain for Hank to call.

She moved out of the hotel at the end of the week and into Charles's house. She met with Ettie and asked her to please stay with her and then she began to pack things away. She and Ettie busied themselves with cleaning out every room in the house throwing away many things the Young's had accumulated in the forty years of their marriage. But she left Ryan's room pretty much the way it was except for the trophies and things that decorated his walls. These she put in cartons and had them stored in the attic. Just in case she and Ryan had a child one of these days, she thought.

For some reason when she thought of Ryan, she could only imagine him whole and healthy. These thoughts gave her strength to wait for the next day. The next day would come and nothing would change. She still could not see Ryan.

Then the event she waited for, for so long happened. Hank called. With the brittle coldness still evident in his voice, he informed Joy that he would be over in thirty minutes and hung up.

Oh, Lord! Please don't let it be more bad news, Joy prayed. Suppose Ryan didn't survive the news of his father's death! Joy paced the room nervously as she waited for Hank's arrival.

Hank arrived with five minutes to spare and Joy was not consoled when she saw him. The coldness she'd detected over the phone was all too real. This was so unlike the warm Hank she remembered of old.

From the minute he walked into the foyer, her defenses were raised. Anyone walking into the room where the two of them stood would immediately detect the tension pervading the area. Walking into the den, Hank gave an obvious snicker. Joy, with hackles raised, noticed his disdain.

"What's wrong with you? See something you don't like?"

Shrugging his wide shoulders Hank spat out, "I just thought you'd have the decency to consult with Ryan before throwing his parents' things out. That's all."

"Oh, and how would I consult Ryan, Mr. Know It All? Remember, you haven't told me where to find him and I, like a fool, promised you I wouldn't look for him until you got back in touch with me. I'm sorry if you don't like what you see, but this is my house now and I will do what I damn well please with it." Joy's anger showed blatantly from her heaving chest to clenched fists.

Hank noticed how the anger caused her face to look flushed. With her cheeks slightly reddened and her eyes shooting golden sparks of anger, she stood there a picture of loveliness. It was all Hank could do to restrain himself from taking her into his arms. He shook his head to clear his mind, trying to change the direction of his thoughts.

Joy noticed the shake and misconstrued it to be one of further disgust. "Hank, let's not…"

As though she hadn't spoken, Hank took up his role as antagonist. "Your house? What about Ryan? Huh? You walked out on him and now that he is rich you expect to just waltz back into his life and take over. How like a woman. Things sure change. I never would have thought you capable of such insensitivity."

"Oh, Hank, give me a break, okay? I really don't give a damn what you think of me and you don't know it all, even if you think you do, so just tell me why you called. Is Ryan okay? Did something happen to him?"

Hank not satisfied by the pain he'd already inflicted on her stabbed her with another barb. "I'm sorry to disappoint you my dear,"

Joy's heart dropped.

"Nothing's happened to Ryan."

Joy let out a sigh of relief and dropped into the nearest chair, for her legs had gone limp.

Seeing the obvious distress she was feeling, Hank felt maybe he'd pushed her too far. Damn her, he couldn't understand her anymore. If he could only know the real reason she was asking for Ryan, he could relax around her more. Letting his defenses down a little, his voice softened just a bit as he walked to the fireplace and placed his arm on the mantle.

"He's holding up, Joy. The news of his daddy's death was devastating for him. They had to sedate him for a couple of days to keep him quite. Now he's just lying there. It seems like he is just willing himself to die. They had to start feeding him intravenously again. He just refuses to eat." Slamming his fist against the mantle he turned to face her. "Damn, I can't even get him to talk to me anymore. It's like all our hard work is going down the drain. We worked so hard to get Ryan where he was. Some of the old Ryan was beginning to surface and now this." Hank's voice trembled as he spoke and Joy detected the tremor of his hand as he ran it through his thick black hair.

He really has been Ryan's truest friend, Joy thought, as she looked at Hank. Involuntarily, she reached out and patted his hand, "It really is rough for you, isn't it Hank? You have stood by Ryan all this time. Not many people have friends like you. Ryan is a lucky man, despite everything he's gone through."

Hank jerked away from Joy and walked across the den where he sat in Charles's big leather recliner. "How in the world can you think that Ryan is a lucky man? If he is considered lucky, keep that kind of luck away from me, lady."

Darn! Joy thought, I've done it again. "Hank, please quit twisting everything I say. You know what I mean, please don't make it into something else." She wanted desperately to ask him if she could see Ryan now, but was afraid to. So, she waited.

After a brief silence from Hank, when he seemed lost in thought, he finally spoke the words she had been waiting to hear. "Joy, if you are determined to see Ryan, I think that maybe you might be the key to bringing him out of this depression. I've spoken to his doctor and he seems to think that perhaps the shock of seeing you might jar him into living again. What do you know of his condition? Do you know what you're walking into?"

"I know about his injuries, if that's what you're asking me. I really don't know what I'm walking into, but I'm sure I can handle it. I've handled worse," she mumbled. Thankfully, Hank didn't hear the last part of Joy's answer because surely he would have become extremely angry.

"Well, if you're sure you want to go through with this, I'm here to bring you to him, but consider yourself warned, lady. If you make a scene and upset him, I will personally drag you out of there. Understood?"

"Understood," Joy spat back. Damn him and his self-righteousness. Vowing not to give him the satisfaction of seeing her break down she gathered her courage and prayed it would serve her well, she grabbed her purse and walked to his car.

# CHAPTER 7

❀

*J*oy sat quietly in Hank's car on the ride to see Ryan. She didn't ask where they were going, she didn't want to upset him in any way and frankly, she no longer knew what would upset him or not. So she just sat there lost in her thoughts.

Hank, too, remained quiet. He was battling his own thoughts and feelings. As he drove, he thought about the past seven years and how he had tried to find someone to take Joy's place in his heart. There had been a few women who had almost succeeded, but before a commitment could be made, he would back out of the relationship.

He was presently seeing Alex and up to a couple of weeks ago, he'd felt he was ready to try the commitment thing. Alex was a nice, sweet woman who had come out of a bad marriage two years ago. She adored Hank and was not afraid to declare her love for him. He truly had begun to think that he loved her too.

Then unexpectedly, Joy walked back into his life and BANG, everything went up in smoke. She was all he could think of for the past couple of weeks. He longed to feel her arms around him and to taste the lips that had haunted him for so long.

Alex was not a stupid woman and had sensed the change in him. She knew she was fighting a losing battle and that it was just a matter of time before he called it quits. She sensed it the minute he introduced Joy to her in his office. After Joy had left his office, Alex had stormed in demanding to know who she really was. That had led to their first major battle because he had not been inclined to talk about her. His evasiveness on the subject of Joy spoke for itself.

Alex felt left out. This was a part of his life he willingly shut her out of and she couldn't handle it; thus an argument had ensued. After the argument he had toyed again with the idea of marrying Alex, hoping maybe that would exorcise his obsession with Joy, but, after all was said and done, he threw the idea out, realizing that marriage to Alex would add to his problems instead of ridding him of them.

Joy was the one he wanted. The only one he had ever wanted. He'd had affairs, but it was always Joy he made love to. In his mind, they were all named Joy. She ran through his veins like blood and nothing could change that. But, for Ryan's sake, he still could not voice his love, no matter how much he wanted to.

It killed him inside when he thought of the hurt look that came into her eyes when he jumped her case, but that was the only way he could handle being with her now. By making her angry with him and convincing her that he disliked her, he could keep her at a distance. He was not able to be "best buddy" to her right now. He was just too vulnerable.

An hour out of New Orleans, they turned onto a tree lined road that led to a sprawling expanse of green grass and large beautiful oak trees, dotted with neat little cottages of various colors. Some were surrounded by white picket fences and were adorned with flower boxes under the front windows. When the full view of the community came into Joy's sight, she gave out an audible gasp.

Hank turned to her and saw the look of awe on her face.

"Yeah, I know, this place gave me the same feeling when I saw it for the first time. Beautiful, isn't it?"

Drawing in her breath, she looked around then exhaled while declaring, "gorgeous, simply gorgeous. It's hard to think of sickness and infirmities in a place like this." Somehow, she felt a little more at ease, seeing that Ryan was in a place so filled with serenity. "How long has Ryan been in this place?" She felt that was a legitimate question and was on safe grounds asking it.

"He's been here for almost seven years. He stayed in the hospital for three months, and then he was brought here."

They were parked beneath one of the majestic oaks and Hank appeared more like the man she remembered. She decided to press her luck and began asking questions, seeking answers she'd often wondered about.

"Hank, when did you find out about the accident? Hadn't you already left for the airport when it happened?"

"Yes, I had left the reception. I really didn't know anything about it until I called home when I reached the base. As a fresh incoming soldier, I wasn't allowed to use the phone but I kept having this feeling that something was wrong. The sensation was so strong, that I paid another new soldier to watch for me as I smuggled in a call home. That's when Mom told me. I can't tell you how badly I wanted to get on the next flight home. I felt like my life had ended too. I held my breath as Momma told me about the accident and all I could ask was if you and Ryan had survived. She told me yes, but wouldn't give any of the details. I suppose she didn't want to upset me more than I already was.

When I came home on leave I found out the extent of Ryan's injuries and that you had left town. I came up here then with Charles and visited with Ryan. I can still remember the first time I saw him after the accident. I could tell he hated that I had to see him like he was. But, after the initial shock wore off, we became comfortable with each other. It was almost like it used to be."

"Almost?"

"Yeah, we still felt the closeness but, I'll be honest with you, we both felt something was missing."

"Missing? What could have been missing? Your friendship knew no boundaries. It encompassed everything. How could something be missing?"

"You're right. Our friendship was special. It always was but then something changed it. It no longer was the same. There was a certain element missing." Briefly looking at her, he said in a voice so low and husky, Joy had to strain to hear it, "I'm talking about you, Joy. You were the missing element. We talked about you a lot at first. It was easier for him to talk back then. Now, he's only able to say a few words at a time. It seems like talking takes too much energy from him."

Joy sat there and listened. She knew Hank needed to talk about all of this and she was relieved that he was confiding in her. She was also relieved to hear that Ryan had talked about her. "Do you think he'll know who I am, Hank? Do you think he'll remember me?"

"There's nothing wrong with his memory Joy. You were Ryan's life. Of course he'll remember you."

He turned to her and placing his hand on her shoulder he asked, "Joy, are you ready?"

Taking a deep breath, Joy looked at Hank and putting a smile on her face she replied, "You bet your fine ass, I am," and got out of the car.

Joy could feel anxiety take over her body as they walked into the foyer of the main hall. Not knowing how Ryan would react when he saw her and not being sure of her reaction as well, was taking its toll on her. She was suddenly very grateful that Hank had called ahead and arranged for her to meet with Ryan's doctor before she saw Ryan for the first time since their wedding day.

The doctor was waiting for her and ushered her into his office, leaving Hank waiting for her in the hall. A part of Joy wanted to haul Hank into the office with her, but another part of her wanted this meeting to be private. Once they began their meeting, Joy was glad she had opted for the latter part of her yearning. She and the man who had taken care of Ryan for the past six and a half years talked for the better part of an hour.

Joy told the doctor the details of her departure from Ryan's life. The doctor sympathetically shook his head from time to time as he listened to her.

He then filled her in on Ryan's condition. He told her that the news of Charles's death had weakened him considerably and that his health had been steadily declining in the past year. He confided in her that someone in Ryan's condition could not expect to live long. The one good thing in Ryan's case was his age and the fact that he was in excellent physical shape at the time of the accident. But, like all things, time has a way of catching up and it seemed that time, for Ryan, was quickly running out.

Joy sat there, motionless except for the flashes of pain in her eyes as she listened to the doctor. Despite what others had told her about Ryan's condition, she had convinced herself they were all exaggerating. And now this doctor was telling her the same thing. Ryan was dangerously close to death.

Joy's mind was reeling with feelings and thoughts. Ryan had just been given back to her, and no one was going to take him away again. She'd convinced herself that Hank and the doctor were continuing the lie that Ryan's parents had started when they'd convinced her to leave New Orleans, only this time they were telling her that he was alive, but not for long. She had decided that she'd believe no one when it came to news about Ryan. She would draw her own conclusions when she saw him. So she listened and heard everything the doctor told her, but her heart and her mind told her otherwise. Ryan was and is a strong, virile man, she told herself again. This time a little more adamantly.

The doctor saw a determined look come over Joy's face and feeling as if he were talking to thin air, he got up from his chair and walked to the door. Joy followed.

As the door to the doctor's office opened, Hank came away from the wall he had been leaning on. Falling in step with them as they walked towards Ryan's room he couldn't help wondering what the doctor had told Joy. He had expected to see her emerge from the office in tears, but she came out with that stupid grin on her face. He thought it was a stupid grin, because it never reached her eyes; it just appeared frozen on her lips.

Reaching the door to Ryan's room, the doctor turned and faced Joy. "I'll wait out here a few minutes, in case you need me, Mrs. Young, that is of course unless you want me to go in with you."

"Thank you doctor. Just knowing you're right outside this door will be a great help." She looked at the doctor and gave him a weak smile. "A part of me is wanting desperately to tell you to come in with me, but a larger part of me knows that I have to do this myself."

He returned her smile with one filled with encouragement. He hoped she was prepared for what she would find. He'd tried to prepare her but felt nothing he said had penetrated her mind. "Be brave, it will be all right," he whispered to her as she placed her hands on the heavy door.

His words were wasted because she couldn't hear him for the pounding of her heart. Anticipation was causing her heart to beat furiously. Before pushing the door open she threw a glance at Hank and for once he saw a glimmer of hesitation.

"Joy, are you sure you're up to this?" he asked again.

Swallowing hard she looked into his eyes and cried, "How do I do this? I feel like I can't just walk in. Oh, Hank suddenly I'm frightened." As she stood there trembling, the color seemed to drain from her face. Her eyes became glazed and she reached for Hank.

Seeing that she was about to fold, Hank reached out and steadied her.

"Joy, you've come this far, you can't back off now. Just open the door and go from there." There was no tenderness in Hank's voice, in fact, the harshness his words held snapped Joy out of her near faint.

She knew Hank was expecting this kind of behavior from her and she feared if she didn't go through the door into Ryan's room Hank would carry her bodily out of the building. Pulling herself together she vowed that she'd prove him wrong. No matter how frightened she was she had waited what seemed an eternity to see Ryan, and see Ryan she would. Today! Now! Joy shot Hank a look that rivaled the harshness in his voice, "thanks for the understanding," she spat sarcastically at him. She drew in a deep breath and pushed the heavy door open and stepped inside.

# CHAPTER 8

T he first thing Joy noticed as she slowly pushed the door open was the color of the walls. They were not the institutional white or green but soft gentle beige. Splashes of light pink, blue and soft green were scattered around the room in the guise of rugs, vases and pictures.

Southwestern, thought Joy, as she felt a lump form in her throat. The southwest had always been Ryan's favorite region. She could see at a glance that Charles had this room specially designed just to suit Ryan. How like him to go to these extremes to make this place more like a home for Ryan. She was relieved that the place did not resemble a hospital room. When Hank told her they'd had to move Ryan to the infirmary at the news of his daddy's death, she'd never imagined the infirmary like this. Then Hank's words echoed in her mind. She'd forgotten that he'd told her that because Ryan was in and out of the infirmary so often, Charles had bought this room especially for Ryan. When Ryan was well enough to be moved, they would move him to one of the attractive bungalows she'd seen scattered over the grounds. But for now, this was his home. She could not stop herself from thinking how different his home would have been, had it not been for the accident.

The next thing she noticed was that his quarters were made up of two rooms and Ryan definitely was not in this one.

To the left Joy could see a large overstuffed leather sofa and chair making up a sitting area. A small round table covered in a green and blue Indian print cloth stood next to the sofa. Pictures of Charles and Mamie were arranged on the table in delicately carved wooden frames. A large throw rug bearing all the colors of the room rested in front of the sofa. Large plate glass windows took up the left wall of the room giving a gracious view of the grounds. The green expanse of well-manicured lawns, the majestic oak trees and delicate white wrought iron benches afforded a delightful view.

Further to the right of the room, landscape pictures adorned the wall. Joy could easily imagine Ryan gazing at them and getting lost in his imagination as he allowed his spirit to enter the deeply wooded mountain scene or fishing in the gently rolling brook that the pictures portrayed. Finally, she focused on a door leading to another room.

Walking to the door she forced her eyes to the center of the room where Ryan was lying in a bed. The bed was larger than most hospital beds but was still easily accessible if need arose. And there, in the center of the bed with eyes closed was the person she loved most in the world.

Ryan!

Joy walked closer to the bed and took advantage of his closed eyes. This gave her time to really look at the person she had longed to see for such a long time and had, up to the past few weeks, given up all hope of ever seeing again.

Her mind raged a battle with her heart as she looked down at the sleeping man. Her mind argued that the man in this bed was not Ryan, could not be Ryan, while her heart screamed out at her, "yes, yes it is." She looked at the man she loved with all her heart and her heart broke. Choking back the sobs, she heard the words; he's just a shell of the man you knew, as they ricocheted in her mind. No! This could not be her Ryan.

Her strong, virile Ryan was a broken, shrunken skeleton of a man. The burns he'd suffered had left the left side of his face covered in scars. Silent tears fell down her face as she took in the puckered scar tissue that replaced his eye and lips on the left side of his face. He had a scar running from the hairline or what had once been his hairline on the right side of his face to below his chin. His neck was uncovered and Joy could see that it, too, was covered with scars. His arms were resting by his sides and although only his hands were visible, Joy imagined them to be covered also with the angry puckering of the scars. Without touching him, she could see the lifelessness of his legs.

She felt the sobs rising in her throat but sensed Hank's presence behind her and knew this was one time she would have to call on her strength to get her through. She knew that if she wanted to stay in here, her tears would have to remain internal, and she knew with all her heart that she did want to stay here, forever, if she could be with Ryan. Quickly, she wiped her tears away with the back of her hand.

Hank moved to the right side of Ryan's bed and watched Joy. He could see the love on her face and it puzzled him even more than the fact that she could stand here and look at him and not shed a tear. If she loved him as much as her eyes said she did, how could she have walked out on him seven years ago and how in the hell could she stand here dry eyed.

Joy raised her head and her eyes locked with Hank's. For a brief moment she thought she saw compassion in his eyes then the coldness returned. Damn him, one minute his eyes are soft and warm and the next they're hard and cold. Well tough, she thought, I'm here with my Ryan now and Hank can just go to hell, if that's what he wants. But deep inside her she knew that was a lie. Hank meant too much to her and to Ryan for her to really have these feelings. She cared what Hank thought, but she couldn't get into that right now. She would deal with that later.

As these thoughts raced in her mind, she saw Hank take Ryan's hand. "Ryan. Ryan, wake up good buddy. It's me, Hank and I've brought you a surprise."

Joy watched as Ryan slowly opened his good eye and tried to smile as he recognized his good friend. The smile quickly vanished as though he had second thoughts about smiling, but Joy saw pain flash in his eyes. God, even a small smile, caused him so much pain. She saw Ryan's pain reflected in Hank's eyes as he returned the somewhat abbreviated smile of his friend. Her eyes met Hank's across the bed as he looked from Ryan to her.

"Turn your head, buddy and get ready for a good surprise. Look what I found on the side of the road," Hank joked.

Ryan slowly turned his head so that Joy would be in his line of vision. He looked at her with a vacant and disinterested look.

Joy held her breath as she watched Ryan turn his head away from her. She could feel her heart shatter as she watched the right side of his mouth move as he tried to say something. Hank bent down to listen to what his friend had to say.

Not being able to take anymore and sure that what Ryan was telling Hank was not good, she moved away from the bedside. She walked to the window trying desperately to quell the tears threatening to spill over. Oh God, maybe Charles had been right. Maybe Ryan didn't want her to see him like this. Perhaps he didn't want to see her at all. Just as she was about to give in to the sudden urge to run out of the room, she heard her name and turned back toward the bed where she saw Hank talking to Ryan. Taking a firm hold on her emotions she convinced herself that if she gave in to the panic rising in her, then she surely would be guilty of running out of Ryan's life. And she was already carrying that accusation. Unfair as it was, Hank still believed she'd run out on Ryan and she suspected he thought she'd run away again. Realizing this, her determination to stay by Ryan's side, no matter what, took root and became firmly planted. Slowly and reluctantly, she walked back to her husband's bedside.

What will I do, she thought, if he doesn't want me here? Please, if there is a God out there, please let me be a part of my husband's life. Please God. Her prayers were so intense; she had not realized she'd closed her eyes.

Suddenly, she heard her name. The sound was raspy and barely audible. Opening her eyes, she found Ryan's gaze on her once again.

"Yes, my love, I'm here," she reached out a shaking hand to touch the man she had so often reached out for in her sleep. She smiled at Ryan. A smile worthy of its recipient. This was a smile completely different from the ones Hank had seen.

This definitely was not one of her stupid smiles, Hank noted. This smile came from deep within her and this one reached her eyes. Hank watched as the dull look in Joy's eyes vanished and was replaced by a brilliant gleam. For a brief second, he felt the jealousy rise, just like old times. No one could make Joy's eyes light up like Ryan did, and Hank was willing to bet this was the first time since the accident that Joy's smile reached her eyes.

Emotions ran high for the next few weeks as Joy and Ryan became reacquainted as best they could. Hank gave Joy and Ryan their privacy, but paid his visit to Ryan once a week as he had for the past three years since his discharge from the army. Although Joy had told Ryan the truth about her departure, she had never told Hank and consequently he still treated her with a distant coldness when they were alone, careful to hide it when in front of Ryan. Thus, the lives of the trio were once again entwined.

Joy's days were spent sitting at Ryan's bedside for hours talking to him. She told him about their stores in L.A. and here in Louisiana. She explained how lonely she was in California and how the memories of what should have been their life haunted her there so she'd come to Shreveport and opened their second store. She talked about Beth and their friendship. She even spoke about Shaze, but not about their involvement and pending marriage. That fact was the only thorn left in her side.

Shaze. What am I going to do about Shaze? She'd asked herself that question a thousand times in the past few weeks. One thing was sure and that was that she could never marry him now. She knew now that she loved Shaze but was not in love with him and now that she knew Ryan was alive she was certain she had no room in her heart for anyone but Ryan. Except maybe for Hank.

When away from the hospital Joy took care of business. She checked on the stores twice a week and was always assured things were going great. When asked about Shaze, Beth would inform her that he'd returned from New Orleans in the best of moods and that he was always away from the store on buying and selling trips. Joy was grateful that things were going so well and that Shaze seemed to be taking all of this in stride.

She still had not told him that Ryan was alive and knew that the time would come when she would have to tell him, only she couldn't do it now. She had just found happiness again and wanted nothing to mar it.

Two weeks after her first visit to Ryan, Joy awakened to a beautiful late summer morning. She rushed into the kitchen and waved away Ettie's offer of breakfast as she quickly downed a cup of cafe a'lait.

"You sure is in a big hurry little missy. What devil is after you dis morning?" Ettie watched Joy gulp her favorite beverage. It sure had been wonderful seeing the joy back in her new boss. Things had changed a great deal and Ettie was grateful that everything had come out in the open about Ryan. It felt so good to be able to talk to someone about her favorite boy. Although Ryan was indeed a man, the old housekeeper still referred to him as her boy.

Joy placed her empty cup on the immaculate counter and kissed the old housekeeper's wrinkled cheek as she passed by her. "Why Miss Ettie, I can't believe you've forgotten what day this is." At the puzzled look on the old lady's face, Joy clucked her tongue and shook her finger at Ettie. "We had better see about giving you a vacation Ettie. Today is Ryan's birthday. He's twenty-six today and I bet he's forgotten about his birthday too."

Ettie clapped her hands over her mouth as she exclaimed, "Bon Dieu, j'obluier," her distress was evident as she repeated herself this time in English bearing her heavy cajun accent. "Good God, I forgot."

Joy began to laugh as she walked back to Ettie and hugged her. "Yes Ettie, God is good and I think he'll forgive you and so will Ryan. You have a good day now, and don't work too hard, because I sure don't want you to forget my birthday. You know it's coming up in a few weeks and you know I certainly won't forgive you if you forget." Ettie pulled her dish towel out of her apron pocket and threw it at Joy as she ran out of the house leaving behind the most delicious laughter Ettie had ever heard.

Joy was filled with excitement as she arrived for her daily visit with Ryan two hours later. She had made a major decision and couldn't wait to tell him about it. It was going to be his birthday present from her. She found him sitting up and looking better than she had since her visits had begun. Kissing him she greeted him, "good morning Darling. Did you have a good night's rest?"

He gave her one of his painful smiles and nodded yes to her question. No matter how much it cost him in pain, he never withheld his smiles from Joy. At first he hated the idea of her visiting him here and seeing him in all of his disfigurement. But now, he looked forward to her daily visits, to her lilting voice as she recounted to him all that he missed in her life. Her presence made him feel like no medicine had ever had the power to. It made him feel strong, young and still handsome. When she looked at him, he was catapulted back in time to the days they had run hand in hand through Jackson Square laughing at the strange sights they encountered. Today was no different. She looked extremely beautiful, all soft and glowing. He felt sadness fill his heart as he took in the sight of her long, soft curls. Oh, how he ached to run his hands through their thick masses. And those lips. He remembered their soft sweetness as he relived every kiss they had ever shared. Well, no matter how much he thought about it, he told himself, he would never be able to twist his hands in her lustrous curls or kiss her lips the way she liked to be kissed. Deep and soft. So, he swallowed hard pushing the sadness away and settled for the happiness he derived from sitting in her presence.

"Ryan, Sweetheart, do you know what day this is?" She sat in the chair next to his bed and he could see excitement radiating from her.

He again shook his head in affirmation and uttered one word. Hank. Today was Hank's visiting day.

Laughing, Joy took his hand. "Yes, today is Hank's visiting day but that's not all. "Come on, think hard. It is a very special day. Silly, today is your birthday."

In her excitement she had not stopped to think that perhaps Ryan would not be as excited about this day as she was.

Ryan lowered his head and would not meet her eyes. Birthday, my birthday, he thought. Big fat deal. What was there to be excited about? Yes, today was his birthday but that was nothing to be excited about. It could possibly be his last according to the doctors. A few weeks ago that would have brought him joy, but now that he had his real joy back, the possibility of him dying soon, saddened him.

"Ryan, did I say something wrong? Darling, look at me, please. Aren't you excited about your birthday? Remember how we used to look forward to our birthdays? We'd rack our brains for the right present to give each other. Remember how each year we tried to make our gifts more special than the year before? This year is no different, love. Please look at me."

Ryan could not ignore the pleading in Joy's voice. He raised his head and met her eyes. "Gift? No special gift this year." His words came slow and labored.

"No special gift? Silly, we have each other. No gift could top that one. I don't know what we'll do for the next ten years, because this year is so special no other gift could come this close to perfection. I promise you, Darling, this will be your best birthday yet." As she spoke she stroked the good side of his face.

"It's been too long Sweetheart, since you've run your hands through my hair." She began to raise his hand to her mass of chestnut curls as she lowered her head to shorten the distance between his hand and her hair. When she felt his hand touching her head, she covered it with hers and caught a handful of the soft curls. Guiding his hand, she drew it away from her head, slowly, letting the curls fall gently through their splayed fingers.

The feel of her curls. What could he compare it to? Like running through fresh green grass barefooted? Like wading through a mountain stream? Perhaps he could compare it to the rush one gets when faced with a large, beautiful waterfall. If only he could do more than just touch her hair, but he couldn't so he'd be satisfied with that. Acceptance of such things had become easier for him through the years and now for the first time his acceptance was tinged with bittersweet regret.

Joy raised her head and met his gaze. A slow smile spread over her face as she saw for the first time since her arrival, a look of lightness enter Ryan's eye. She still held a mischievous glint in her eyes as she gave him a sly wink. "How do you like your birthday, so far? Pretty good, huh?"

He gave a wobbly smile that was larger than usual, causing him to wince a little more than usual. He saw Joy's eyes cloud with worry immediately. Wishing to diminish her worry, he smiled again, this time using much of his dwindling energy to hide the evidence of pain. "Great birthday," he panted.

Joy leaned over and kissed him. Not just a kiss on the right corner of his mouth where there was no scar tissue. This time she kissed him full on the lips. At first with just a gentle touching of the lips, then gradually she increased the pressure. Just a little. Not enough to cause him any pain, but enough to let him feel kissed. Her eyes were closed and for a brief time, she too was transported back to the days when everything was perfect. Then she felt wetness touch her cheek. Tears. It had to be tears. She didn't want to cry, not today. Today was to be their perfect day. Just laughter. No tears, and here she was crying.

She opened her eyes and saw the tears were coming from Ryan's closed eyes. They were his tears, not hers. Her eyes grew large with concern, "did I hurt you? Oh, my God. Ryan, did I push this too far? I knew I shouldn't have kissed you like that, but Darling I felt that was what you wished for, for your birthday. Do you want me to call the nurse?"

The look of concern mixed with the look of her love for him was almost more than he could bear. Shaking his head from side to side he whispered, "no pain just gratitude. Thank you, love."

Not being able to hold back her tears of love, Joy leaned over and kissed him once more. Neither of them heard the door open. Neither of them saw the pained look in Hank's eyes as he slowly backed away from the open door and gave them a few minutes more of privacy.

Hank returned a few minutes later with a stack of compact discs for Ryan to listen to. "Couldn't forget your birthday, good buddy," he'd told Ryan as he placed the discs on the table next to the player. "Seeing the twinkle in your eye, I suppose my gift is strained green beans compared to Joy's gift, huh?" He looked at the glowing couple and winked causing Joy and Ryan to laugh.

The afternoon was perfect. The weather was simply gorgeous and Joy thought of a splendid idea. She convinced Hank to help her move Ryan's bed so he could enjoy a better view of outside. The afternoon was crystal clear with the sky boasting a dome of brilliant blue dotted with high puffs of white clouds. Birds were in abundance as they danced in the birdbaths and sang their love songs.

The three of them sat. Sometimes talking, sometimes quite, lost in each their own thoughts.

The sun had a soothing effect on Ryan, shedding gentle beams of light on him as it coaxed him to sleep embraced in its gentle warmth. He slept peacefully. It was so good to have both Joy and Hank together with him. Just like old times. He always dreamed of the old times but lately the dreams were turning sour. As hard as they tried to hide it from him, some distance had come between Hank and Joy. He did not know what was causing the dissention between them, but he knew it was there. He could feel it and he did not like it. He'd have to do something about it. But not today. Today had to be perfect.

"Joy, my darling, you were so right. This has been my best birthday ever." He said the words, but she couldn't hear them. They were spoken, but only in his mind, in his dream.

When Ryan next opened his eyes, Joy was still sitting next to his bed, a magazine waiting to be picked up and read lay in her lap. Hank could not be seen in his line of vision. "Hank?"

The word brought Joy out of her reverie. "Hank had some errands to take care of. He told me to tell you he'd see you next week. Same day, same time."

Ryan nodded slowly and lifted his hand in Joy's direction. Sensing he was afraid she'd be leaving too, Joy picked up his extended hand. "It's okay, Sweetie, I'm not leaving. We still have time today." His anxiety began to ebb and Joy watched as his tenseness gave way to gentle relaxation. Now, Joy thought, now is the time for me to tell him of my decision. Giving his hand a gentle squeeze, Joy began. "Darling, you know we've spoken before of the possibility of selling the L.A. store and making New Orleans my permanent residence again. How do you truly feel about that? Would it make you happy to have me with you again, everyday like we'd planned?" She swallowed the lump of fear caused by her anticipation of the answer to her next question. "Or, were your parents right, and you don't really want me here with you?"

At first Ryan attempted a smile. The day had been long, and although he'd enjoyed every bit of it, he was becoming wearied. But as her questions took on the tone of her uncertainty about his feelings, he grew agitated. His face hardened at the mention of his parents' ploy to keep her away from him. His one good eye shot golden daggers. He tried to talk but Joy could see the effort it took.

Frightened that she'd made him too agitated, she placed her cheek on his hand and cooed, "Shh It's all right, Darling. I've made a decision." She raised her head meeting his gaze. She placed her hand on his chest and was alarmed at the furious pounding of his heart. Quickly, she went on, "Love, I'm going to go ahead with my plans to sell." She sensed his approval immediately and was grateful to feel the slowing of his terrified heart. She sat there for the rest of the afternoon talking to him about the plans she needed to make. Ryan seemed contented with this arrangement as he lay there trying never to take his eyes off her. Throughout the afternoon, the effort to stay awake was too much and he'd drift off in a nap. But Joy never stopped. Even while he slept, she talked to him in soft tones. After all, they had so much lost time to make up for. Eventually, sunlight was replaced by the soft glow of floor lamps in Ryan's room and Joy had to leave once again. Kissing her husband good night, she was satisfied that her goal for the day had been achieved. Surely, this was the best birthday Ryan had ever had.

Later that night, alone in her bed she allowed the memories of the past to surface. It still broke her heart to see the young, strong man she remembered and loved so much replaced by a decimated shell of his former self.

The explosion of the car and the reason behind the explosion began to nag at her. When she'd asked Hank about it, he'd told her simply that it had been regarded as a malfunction in the car and nothing had been done about it. An insurance investigation had taken place, but the explosion had destroyed the car and no other conclusions had been drawn. It went down in the records as a malfunction, the insurance company settled with Charles and that was that.

A malfunction. Joy repeated the word out loud, disliking even the sound the word made. Their lives were destroyed and all anyone could say was that is was caused by a malfunction. There had to be more to this, she thought as she began to pace the room. She was dissatisfied with the answers she'd gotten and knew in her gut, that there had been nothing wrong with the car. After all, the day of the wedding had not been the first time the car had been driven. Why would some "malfunction" wait until their wedding day to surface? No, no one would be able to convince her that a car malfunction caused all this misery. Thoughts of the explosion kept nagging at her but try as she might, she just couldn't figure it out. She could think of no one that hated Ryan or her enough to want to harm them or possibly kill them.

One day, she vowed, one day I will get to the bottom of this, and I promise, whomever was responsible for this will pay, if it is within my power. That promise was to herself as well as to Ryan and it stayed in her mind always, just below the surface of normal thought.

# CHAPTER 9

⚜

*T*he days flew by and the nights dragged on. Having reached the decision to sell the L.A. store Joy faced her next step, going back to Los Angeles. Going back meant leaving Ryan. It also meant having to face Shaze. Caught between the two, she didn't know which she hated the most. Leaving Ryan or facing Shaze. I have to go back soon, she argued with herself. No matter how much she hated the idea, she knew that if she didn't go, Shaze would probably show up in New Orleans. The thought of that gave her the shivers. Now that she knew Ryan was alive, she didn't want Shaze anywhere near her.

Then the inevitable happened. Shaze called. She had just returned from the hospital. Her visit had been one of the good ones and she was in a happy frame of mind as she answered the phone. Her heart immediately dropped as she heard his deep throaty voice. God, how long had it been? Try as she might she could not remember the last time she'd spoken to him. Grateful he called instead of showing up, Joy softened her voice as she spoke his name.

It had been a long time, but Shaze carefully guarded his tone. He did not want any of his agitation and frustration coming through. It had been well over a month since he'd agreed to postpone the wedding and left Joy in New Orleans, and he was ready to pick up the pieces of their lives. Tonight, he'd force Joy into giving him a date marking her return to L.A. and to him. But for now, he warned himself, he'd have to take it easy. For if he angered her, he knew it would push her away and he would have to go to New Orleans to get her. That was something he really didn't want to do. He wanted to stay away from New Orleans unless he absolutely had to return.

His conversation at first was general. He was full of good news concerning the stores, telling her he had tripled their orders of the past six months. Joy ran her jewelry business a little differently than most of Charles's other stores. She bought from manufacturers as well as designed some of her own and she sold wholesale as well as to the public. Tripling their orders of the past six months was no little task.

She thanked Shaze and was telling him the truth when she said that she was proud of his accomplishments.

Then he asked the dreaded question, "Why haven't you come home yet?"

Before she could answer, he threw her another question.

"Is there a problem with the inheritance?"

"No, there isn't a problem, but you know how much red tape is involved in these things." Her voice hardened and Shaze knew he'd blown it anyway. "I'm afraid it might be a while longer before I can come back." She had a feeling he was more concerned about the inheritance than he was about her.

Damn, stupid fool. His opinion of himself at this point was low. Real low. Maybe if I change my tone, he thought as he lowered his voice and allowed a touch of infantile begging to enter, "not even for a weekend? Aw love, I miss you terribly. I need to see you. Soon. Do you think you might be able to come home next week?" Damn, let it work, he repeated over and over in his mind as he pled with her to return. He hated demeaning himself like this. Begging for a visit from his fiancée. But if that's what it took for her to come back, he'd do it. "Just for a day or two, after all, you can afford to. Besides, you know we need to finalize our wedding plans. I don't know how much longer I can wait. It seems like I've waited forever for you to become Mrs. Shaze Martin."

Joy froze. How in the world was she to tell him that she could not marry him. For some reason, she just couldn't bring herself to tell him that her husband was living. Just the thought of Shaze finding out about Ryan, caused a heavy feeling deep inside her stomach and a cold chill to run through her body. It was because of these feelings that she'd withheld the news from Beth too. The thought of Shaze finding out about Ryan from someone other than herself caused her to shudder; yet she couldn't tell him.

"I'll see what I can do, Shaze. I'll talk to the attorney but really, so much has to be done. We have to put everything on my name now, and oh, it's really too much to talk about. I don't know all of the legalities involved, but I do know they're time consuming." Joy's voice sounded tired, but he failed to pick up on that fact.

"Honestly, Joy? Are you really going to try to arrange it?" He wanted to sound elated, but he sounded doubtful. His desire was too strong. It was eating him up and he was too consumed by it to realize it was happening.

"I told you I would. What's wrong, don't you trust me anymore?" She was tired of his adolescent behavior and wanted this conversation to end but he continued.

"I'll always trust you. You know that. I've already told you I'm anxious to make you my wife and I can't do that with you on the other side of the country. Dammit, I'm lonesome."

The petulance in his voice grew and Joy wanted desperately to shout out at him to shut up. The urge to tell him to grow up was overwhelming as she listened to his whining. He sounded like a spoiled little boy who could not get his way. It was not the first time he'd sounded like that and Joy could not believe that she'd once considered it charming. Tonight, it was anything but charming and it was getting to her. Instead of voicing her thoughts, she held her breath and silently prayed to her darling Ryan for forgiveness as she lied to Shaze.

"I'm lonesome too and I want to be over there with you, but we have to be patient. Just a little while longer, I promise. Okay?"

Reluctantly, Shaze gave in. "Okay, but if I don't see you in the next two weeks, I'm coming down. Got that? Two weeks, not a second more."

"Okay, Shaze, okay. Two weeks," she agreed. She forced herself to listen as he made idle conversation for a few minutes more. Finally, he rang off saying he had someone ringing his doorbell.

Gratefully, Joy hung up the phone, realizing that Shaze was floating so high he never noticed that he did most of the talking and that she had not said I love you.

Early the next morning Joy arrived at the hospital to find Ryan in terrible pain. He'd taken a turn for the worse during the early morning hours. Forced oxygen was helping him to breathe and she could see the laborious and shallow movement of his chest. Fever was wracking his frail body and hallucinations had taken over.

Joy sat there while numbness invaded her being. She had never thought of the nightmares Ryan might have because of the explosion. Here he was, flailing his arms and trying to scream out to her. She could hear her name coming from deep within him and she could see the fear on his face as he relived the explosion.

Sobbing, all she could do was hold his hand and try to reassure him. "Ryan, my love, I'm here. Darling, it's okay, it's over. Ryan, please hear me. No one can hurt you anymore."

His only response to her assurances was guttural supplications of "Joy! Where is my Joy? Help her. Save Joy," and renewed thrashing of his body while it shuddered from the force of his screams and his despair.

Helpless, Joy sat there pleading with the nurses as they came in to check his vitals. "Help him, please. Can't someone do something?" Only to be met with sympathetic looks from the nurses and their replies of, "I'm sorry, Mrs. Young, there is nothing more we can do. It's out of our hands now." Oh, how Joy had become to hate those dismal words.

Looking down at Ryan, she began to sense what Charles and Mamie had tried desperately to spare her. Watching someone you love, die a slow and agonizing death was pure hell.

Still, she sat there murmuring her soft reassurances in the hopes that her words would reach him even if only in a brief moment of lucidness. "I'll not give up, Ryan, but you have to fight too. Help me to help you. I love you. Please don't leave me," she begged as tears coursed down her cheeks.

Wrapped in her fear for Ryan's life, she was unaware of Hank, until he lightly touched her shoulder. Jumping to her feet, she threw her arms around his neck. "Hank, oh Hank, I'm so glad you're here. I'm losing him, what can I do? I can't stand it. I can't lose him, I can't lose him." The pounding of her fists on Hank's broad chest emphasized the last words.

Hank summoned the nurse and asked her to stay with Ryan for a few minutes then he led the distraught Joy out of the room. "Let's go for a walk, Joy. You need a change of scenery." Hank knew very well what she was going through, for he had experienced it several times too. Ryan's health was so frail, the slightest infection could bring him to the brink of death but then his courage and determination would take over and he would get better. Hank explained this to Joy and she looked up at him with gratitude filling her eyes as she clutched to the string of hope he threw her. They walked hand in hand, not speaking, both lost in their thoughts.

An hour later they returned to Ryan's room and found a much more peaceful Ryan. The nurse met them at the door and putting her arms around Joy she reassured her, "Mrs. Young, his fever has broken. He'll be okay. He's made it." Looking up at Hank, the nurse winked and said, "once again."

Hank smiled at the nurse, winked back and turned to Joy, "See, what did I tell you?"

Joy, crying happily now from relief, hit Hank with the open palm of her right hand, "for once, I'm glad you knew what you were talking about, Mr. Know It All," she said as she returned to Ryan's side. She smoothed the damp strands of hair from his forehead and leaned down to place a kiss on his lips as she whispered, "thank you and welcome back my darling." He responded with a weak smile as a tear slid down his cheek.

Joy left the hospital later. Much later. She would not think of leaving until she was reassured by Ryan's doctor that he was okay, for the time being. And for the first time, she left frightened. Frightened that the day would soon come when her good night kiss would be the last one she'd give to Ryan.

Dwelling on the aspect of Ryan's death was no good for Joy and she knew it. To dispel the fear she felt she began to think of Shaze's call the night before. She knew she needed to go back to tie things up in her old life but at the same time, she knew she could not leave Ryan. Suppose she left even for a day or two, and they'd have a repeat of today. If Ryan died while she was away, she'd never be able to forgive herself.

If it weren't for having to settle things with Shaze, she would not have to worry about leaving now. She could have Beth continue to run the store until she could get away. Shaze. The source of her trouble. Why? Why did I let myself get involved with Shaze? she asked herself. The answer blared back at her.

"You wanted children and your biological clock was ticking away. Family, you've always wanted a family of your own and Shaze, well; Shaze is a good-looking guy. He's intelligent and he'd indicated his desire to settle down and become a family man. Remember, Joy, how he made you feel so comfortable at a time you felt like a wanderer? That my girl is why you got involved. Okay, but that still doesn't help me now. How am I going to get out of this?"

This conversation with herself was an old and often repeated one. When things began to crowd her, she would revert to conversations with her psyche. Sometimes the conversations would help her find a solution but today, it left her empty and more confused.

Later at home, she poured herself a glass of wine and pondered the situation again. Still arriving at no suitable conclusion, she gave up and brought her wine glass and the decanter to the bedroom. She turned the radio on and tuned it to an oldies station. Kicking off her shoes she poured herself another drink then stretched out across the bed. Ryan. Shaze. Ryan. Shaze. Hank. They all intermingled in her mind losing her in the confusion. Finally, she gave up the fight and let her emotions take over. The sobs came from deep within but offered her little relief. She cried and she drank. Soon, the glass she held in her hand was empty and she fell into an exhausted and troubled sleep.

The room was dark when she awakened later to the insistent ringing of the doorbell. Ettie will get it, she mumbled then remembered she'd given Ettie a couple of days off to visit a sick sister. Not taking time to refresh herself, she stumbled to the door to see who was impatiently sitting on the buzzer and found Hank with a worried and frantic look in his eyes.

Immediately, Joy raised her hand to cover her mouth as she hoarsely whispered, "Ryan? Has something happened to him?" while gripping the doorknob with her other hand to steady herself.

Seeing her fear, Hank realized she had misread the worry in his eyes. She caused the worry. He had been standing there ringing the doorbell for twenty minutes before she'd answered the door. Before he could tell her Ryan was still holding his own, her face lost its color and she crumbled to the floor.

Hank reached down and picked up the slight form of the woman he'd loved for most of his life. Her body was petite and he felt her vulnerability in the slightness of her weight. He was always so enervated by her presence; he'd never paid attention to the fact that she'd lost weight since her arrival. In fact, Joy had lost fifteen pounds in the month she'd been back in New Orleans.

Hank felt his heart break as he gently placed her on the sofa in the family room. He placed a gentle kiss on her lips, and then went in search of a wet washcloth to place on her forehead. He sat there, cradling her in his arms and gently patting her face with the cloth until she came to.

The first thing she felt were the strong, gentle arms holding her. "Ryan" she whispered as she stroked the arm around her waist. She felt the muscular arms tighten around her. Opening her eyes she saw a shadow of pain cross Hank's face

"No, darling. It's not Ryan. It's me, Hank. Joy, you fainted before I could tell you that Ryan is still holding his own. He's okay for now love. You can relax. Keep your strength, Joy, because you may have to go through this many times." For once his voice was soft and affable.

"Oh, Hank! When I saw you at the door, you had such a look of despair, I just knew you were bringing me bad news." Turning in his arms so that she faced him, Joy asked, "If Ryan is okay, why did you look so worried? You scared me to death."

"I'm sorry I scared you, love. I promise you that was not my intention. I knew you'd had a bad day at the hospital today and I thought I'd come check on you. You know, see if you were okay and everything." He lowered his head as though embarrassed at his concern. In mock anger he gently shook her, "I rang the damn doorbell for the better part of twenty minutes. I knew you were here, because I could hear music playing and your car was in the garage, but you wouldn't answer the door. I got scared and that was what you saw in my eyes. Fear and worry yes, but not because of Ryan.

This is so hard for you, baby and I hate like hell to see you go through it."

Pulling Joy to him he began stroking the back of her head. He could feel the silkiness of her luxuriant chestnut hair and the scent of her penetrated his deepest recesses.

Her arms wrapped around his neck on their own accord as she nestled her face in the hollow of his neck.

He could feel the warmth of her breath as she cried softly. He held her there; in a bittersweet embrace bringing him exultation to have her in his arms and bitter sorrow because all he could do was comfort her in this brotherly fashion.

Joy felt her arms wrap around Hank's neck and could not stop them. She felt so safe and warm. It had been such a long time since anyone had held her this way. Not demanding. Not expecting anything in return. Just holding her to comfort her. So unlike Shaze, she thought. He held her too, but it inevitably ended up with her putting up with his roving hands. He never held her this way. The way Ryan used to.

Ryan! Coming to her senses, she pulled away from Hank, but not before she felt the beating of his heart next to hers.

His eyes were still filled with softness as he watched her get up and walk to the bar across the room.

Feeling the barriers down between them, Joy decided to seek Hank's advice. Pouring them each a glass of wine, she told him she felt she needed to go away for a few days but that she hated to leave Ryan. He told her that he understood her need to check on the stores; after all, she did have responsibilities. It felt so wonderful to have him to lean on. He seemed so understanding and so much like the Hank she remembered. The soft gentle one, not the hard condescending one she'd returned to find. This coupled with the stress of having to end the relationship with Shaze, had Joy on the brink of tears.

Hank noticed the tears swelling in her eyes.

"Why are you crying, Joy? Is there something I can do, love? Did I say something to upset you?"

Joy gave him one of her special smiles, "no, Hank you've done nothing to upset me. On the contrary you have helped me so much. Just being here and letting me lean on you is more than I expected. I was just thinking how nice it is right now between us. It feels almost like old times. I hate it when I see you look at me with coldness and hatred. You've never hated me before, at least I don't think you ever did, and I can't remember doing anything to change that. Then I come home and see you for the first time in years and am met with this loathing," Joy trembled as she wrapped her arms around herself.

It took all Hank had to keep from jumping up and taking her in his arms. Choking back his declaration of love for her he replied instead, "I don't hate you Joy. Never in my life have I hated you. Things change, people change and I guess the past years have just separated us more than we expected." It was a feeble answer but it was the best he could manage for now.

"Thank you for telling me you don't hate me and I suppose you're right about people changing. Anyway, it's been a long time since someone held me so tenderly, just for the sake of holding me, and I guess I got sentimental."

The conversation was flowing naturally between them, as Joy refilled their wine glasses. The first drink turned into the second and then became a third. It was at this time that Joy slipped and mentioned Shaze.

Hank stiffened up instantly. Slamming his glass on the table he shouted, "What? What did you say? Why do you have to leave?"

Before Joy could explain further, he began hurling accusations in her direction. "Great, Joy! Just great." Shaking his head he looked at her with disgust. "Old habits are hard to break I suppose. Was it fun playing the martyr for a while? The poor concerned wife." His eyes blazed and the fury that shown from them imprisoned Joy so that she was unable to move. "I should have known it was all a show. The going is getting rough, so now you want to run away again. Tired of the games you've been playing? You're ready for some fun now, so you'll run back to your lover. Yeah, I bet it's the store you're worried about." Disgust replaced the anger in his voice as he shouted, "Why didn't you just come out and tell me straight, that you had another man waiting for you? No, instead you hang around getting all you can while inside you can't wait to run to some man's arms. I never took you to be the bitch you really are."

Joy jumped to her feet with eyes blazing and hands balled up into fists. Facing Hank she shouted, "Shut the hell up, you egotistical bastard. Are you so damned perfect that you can sit here and judge me? You don't know the first of anything in my life and I wish to hell you would stop presuming that you know me so damn well."

Hank grabbed her uplifted arm and grasping her wrist in his hand he demanded to know who this bastard, Shaze was.

Joy, angry beyond words now, told him that Shaze was the man she was engaged to. She was so angry, she didn't care if he believed that she was still considering marrying Shaze or not.

Hearing that she was engaged and he was about to lose her to another man again, he lost his composure. Pulling her to him he crushed her body next to his while his lips sought hers. He would not lose her before he kissed her. Just this once. His desire was urgent and his kiss reflected it.

Incensed by his audacity, Joy fought him, but soon her struggles subsided and she began to respond. Her tongue met his as they searched out each other. Hank groaned and pulled Joy closer to him. His hands were exploring the mounds and valleys he'd so often dreamed of.

Her fingers clutched at his hair as the curls came up and wrapped around her fingers. She felt the strength of his muscles as he strained to pull her as close as he could. As the kiss deepened Joy slowly became aware of the warmth spreading through her. It felt so good. Too good. She had to stop this, but how? She didn't want it to ever quit. Hank must be feeling the same way, she thought, as she felt the pounding of his heart as it beat in tune with hers. Just as Joy realized the beating had become as one, Hank moved his lips to the hollow of her neck. Slowly he left a trail of warmth as his lips moved from her neck to behind her ear.

"My God, how I love you," his voice was heavy with desire.

Just then Ryan's face came into focus and she heard his labored declaration of love. The guilt was too much for Joy to bear.

Hank felt her body go limp. She felt lifeless, like a rag doll in his arms. Joy had fainted. Hank carefully picked her up and brought her to the bedroom. "Darling, I know you were overwhelmed, but your timing leaves a lot to be desired." He joked but inside, he knew the reason she fainted. Guilt. She felt guilty because she enjoyed the kiss they'd shared. I wonder if you faint when this Shaze fellow kisses you, he thought. Softly he asked, "How can you feel guilty about kissing me when you are planning to marry someone else?" Did she feel guilty because of her betrayal of Ryan or was it because of her new love? Shaking his head he muttered, "women, who understands them" and tenderly placed her on the bed.

Seeing her lying there with no color in her face he immediately felt sorry for having placed more strain on her by kissing her, but he had waited patiently for so long and then to hear that she had another man in her life just tore him apart and he'd lost control. His body shuddered with the sheer desire to possess her as he stood looking down at her.

Reaching out, he passed his hand over the silken brown curls that framed her face. It felt like it looked, just like silk. He lovingly pushed it back from her face and gasped as he saw the reason for the new hairstyle. A ragged scar ran from the top of her head, near the hairline on the left side of her face, down to just above her jaw line. The scar wasn't too noticeable because it ran close to the hairline and ear and her hair, when worn down, covered it. Hank looked at the scar, amazed at its resemblance to Ryan's. "Damn," he swore, "these two are made so perfectly for each other, they even share some of the same disfigurements."

Hank stood there soaking in the sight of Joy. He could see tears slip through her closed eyes. He leaned down and softly urged her to sleep as he assured her that everything would be all right. He watched as she curled up like a small frightened child clutching the coverlet to her chin as though for protection. Slowly he turned and walked softly out of the room.

Joy slept, but not peacefully. She dreamed of being alone with Hank. They were kissing. Then the room would fill up with images of Ryan crying and gasping for breath and Shaze shaking his fist, shouting obscenities at her.

She awakened an hour later to the sound of thunder rumbling in the distance and a knock on her door. Giving permission to come in, Joy watched as Hank entered carrying two cups of coffee. She struggled to sit up. Her hair, dampened by the tears shed in her sleep, was still pushed away from her face. Seeing Hank's eyes go briefly to her scar, she quickly ran her hand through the tangled mass bringing it down to cover the left side of her face. Without a word she reached up and took one of the cups from Hank then watched as without a word to her he walked into the adjoining bathroom. Before Joy could find her voice, she heard water running in the tub. What do you think he's up to now, she wondered. Something had happened before, but all she could remember was Hank and her fighting. How did I get in my bed, she wondered, as she sipped her coffee? Then she remembered being in Hank's arms. My Lord! How far did they go? Joy looked down and saw that she was still fully dressed. Trembling she placed the empty cup on her nightstand and reached up to cradle her aching head in her hands. They were shaky but not as much as her insides were.

Hank emerged from the bathroom smiling shyly at her. "Maybe you'll feel better after a hot bath. I've run one for you. Take your time. I'll be waiting for you in the den. We'll finish our conversation if you're up to it." He walked to the bed, bent down and gently placed a kiss on the top of her head. He straightened up and walked out of the room, pulling the door closed behind him.

# CHAPTER 10

$\mathcal{J}$oy got out of bed and carefully walked to the bathroom. Her legs were weak and she was trembling from head to toe. Too much, too fast, she thought, and wondered what those words meant. Was she talking about Shaze, Ryan, Hank or the wine? Like I thought, she said to herself as she climbed into the tub, too much, too fast.

Joy soaked in the tub of warm bubbles for what seemed to her, hours but in fact was just a matter of minutes and emerged from the tub feeling refreshed. She'd had time to think about what had happened between her and Hank and decided that is was perfectly natural. It was just a kiss born of frustration and high levels of stress. Yet, the memory of the kiss stayed vividly with her.

She walked into the den and found it empty, but she could hear sounds coming from the kitchen. Hank was at the stove stirring something that smelled delicious. She glanced around the room taking in the table set for two, complete with candles.

Hank looked up from the pot he'd been stirring when he heard her enter the room. "Uh, I hope you still like crawfish etouffe," he commented as he poured the etouffe in one of her crystal bowls. He looked away without really meeting her eyes. He was ashamed of his behavior of before.

"Do I still like crawfish etouffe? Are you crazy? No one stops liking something that good." Joy was determined to keep the mood light.

She sensed Hank was feeling guilty about their shared kiss and this dinner was his way of apologizing. She had come to terms with her guilt while in the bath and could admit now that she didn't mind the kiss, but she hated the arguing they always seemed to get into.

The crawfish were cooked to perfection and Hank had prepared a bowl of steaming rice to go along with it. A crisp green salad with poppy seed dressing and hot baked rolls rounded out his menu. Joy was quite impressed with Hank's culinary talents and told him so.

"This is great. How and when did you become an expert in the kitchen?"

"When you've lived alone as long as I have, you learn to cook and when you have to eat your own cooking you make sure it's good," he shrugged his shoulders, "I guess it's in the Cajun heritage. I believe we are born with a natural instinct for preparing great culinary delights."

"I suppose I'd have to agree with you," she responded playfully, "because I make a mean meal or two myself."

They continued the meal with light banter between them and Hank couldn't help but feel the rightness of it all. They belonged together. He was sure of that, but he reminded himself of the fact that the woman sitting across the table from him was his best friend's wife. She was a vision of angelic beauty as she sat there. The glow from the candlelight enhanced her soft feminine features. Her thick chestnut hair reflected the golden hues cast from the flickering candlelight and her eyes shone like black diamonds. She was dressed in a white crinkly cotton dress that flowed softly around her exquisitely shaped body, adding to the already ethereal look she portrayed.

It was difficult for Hank to keep his thoughts pure as he gazed at her from across the table. I have no business thinking of her this way, he admonished himself, but then again, in the matters of the heart, who can control such thoughts?

As Joy wiped her mouth and placed her napkin on the table, Hank picked up the coffee carafe and poured her a cup of coffee.

"Umm, this is one of the things I've missed most while I was away," she cooed as she savored the steamy fragrance. "There is nothing like good Creole coffee."

"Is that all you missed while you were away, Joy?" Hank asked as he placed his hand on hers, half expecting her to draw it away.

Contrary to his thought, Joy did not pull away. Instead she sat there looking down at his hand covering hers and scarcely shaking her head from side to side. Bringing her eyes to meet his, she inhaled deeply then whispered slowly, "No, that's not all that I've missed, Hank. I've missed seven years of my life. I've missed my friends, my lovely New Orleans and my husband."

Hank said nothing. For once words failed him. He sat there lost in the vast darkness of her eyes.

She returned his look and felt a tingling sensation run through her like an electric shock. Damn, he's so good looking, she thought. He had tiny fingers of gray creeping in at his temple then getting lost in the blackness of his thick hair. The gray intensified the grayness of his eyes. His face was deeply tanned with tiny laugh lines in the corners of his eyes indicating his usually jovial mood. A mood Joy saw little of since her return. She knew only so well how the twinkling could easily turn into hardness as his moods changed. Her eyes traveled slowly down his face taking in his straight nose and full lips topped by a closely cropped salt and pepper moustache. A well manicured, short-cropped beard covered his cheeks and chin. Her gaze stopped at his shoulders, which seemed to stretch across the room and she remembered how strong and solidly built his muscles were as he'd held her next to him. I've got to stop this, she silently scolded herself. It didn't work. The idea of this virile, sexy man being so close to her was unnerving. She tried again by reminding herself that she was a married woman and this handsome guy was her husband's best friend, but to no avail. She couldn't shake the feeling that this was meant to be. But it couldn't. Hank was the third member of the "trio" and could be no more than that. Tearing her eyes from Hank's she told herself she had enough to take care of without complicating her life more by having these thoughts about him.

"Hey, earth to Joy, are you still in there?"

Joy came out of her thoughts to see Hank waving his hand in front of her eyes. Shaking her head a little to clear it, she laughed, "Yeah, I'm still here. Got lost in thoughts, that's all."

Hank knew better than to ask what kind of thoughts she'd been lost in. He had a pretty good idea what they were as he looked at her flushed cheeks.

They remained at the dinner table and Hank was the first to bring up the subject of her planned departure.

He tried to keep his voice devoid of emotion. "Okay, love, let's talk about your trip. When do you propose to leave?"

Afraid they'd have a repeat of their earlier conversation Joy replied hesitantly, "I don't know. I've spoken to Ryan about it and he seemed somewhat agitated when I mentioned leaving. Do you think he'll be okay while I'm gone?" She was afraid of his reaction to her concern for Ryan.

But now her fear was unfounded. Hank's voice held a hint of resignation in it as he said, "it's hard to say, Joy. Now that you are back in his life, I think he'll...hell, I don't know what he'll think or do."

"Hank, if he doesn't want me to go, I won't."

"But, if you don't, what will you do about this other guy? What was his name again?"

Joy held her breath. Here it goes again, she thought. But again, Hank surprised her with his composure.

"Tell me about him Joy, where did you meet him and what is he like?" Hank's voice was steady. Emotionless.

Joy inhaled deeply, and looked down at her hands as they lay curled into balls in her lap. "Shaze," the word was barely audible. "His name is Shaze Martin. He came into the store one day looking for a job. His resume was impressive and his references checked out. I had an opening and he needed a job, so I hired him. He's really been good for the stores, Hank." Her eyes begged him for under-standing. "The customers all like him, especially the women." Joy smiled slightly as she vocalized this last attribute. Yes, he was quite a lady's man, she thought, and this lady fell like a lead pipe. She con-tinued, "we spent a lot of time together because of the stores and I guess our working relationship grew into a friendship. Shaze is so easy to get along with," almost as an afterthought she added, "most of the time. With me anyway. He and Beth, now that's another story."

Hank took Joy's hand back into his and looking her straight in the eyes asked, "Joy, do you love him?"

Returning his look directly, she answered, "Yes, well, at that time, I did love him. It wasn't like the love I had for Ryan, but it was love. I knew that I could never love another man in the way I loved Ryan, but Shaze loved me and I desired marriage and children, so I figured, why not?"

Hank's eyes reflected pain but before Joy could remark on it, he asked more questions. "What do you know about his background?"

"Very little. He was reared by his mother somewhere in south-western Louisiana. That was another reason I hired him. He was a fellow from home." Again, her eyes took on this look that screamed for understanding. "His father, as I recall him saying, was killed in an automobile accident when he was a small boy. He remembered his father and spoke about him often. He's from the south but hasn't talked much about his hometown."

"So, he's a good ole Cajun boy? Just where in the south does he come from?"

Joy couldn't fail to recognize the sarcasm in his voice. Gone was the absence of emotion. His jealousy was unmasked and he didn't seem to care.

Joy retorted, "I wouldn't go so far as to say he's Cajun, unless he's lost his accent along the way. He's from somewhere in southwestern Louisiana, but honestly Hank, I can't remember if he ever told me exactly where." Tiring of this subject, Joy arose from the table and walked into the den.

Following her, Hank finally asked her the question he dreaded, "are you going to go through with your plans to marry him?"

Spinning on her heels, Joy turned and gave him a hurt and bewildered look. "How can you ask me that? You know I can't marry Shaze. I am still married to Ryan, remember, and have no intention of getting out of this marriage, although it is a marriage in name and spirit only."

Joy's answer took Hank by surprise, "what changed things? You knew you were married when you became involved with Shaze. Nothing's changed. Why aren't you going to marry him now?"

Turning from the window she'd been gazing out of, Joy faced Hank. "You really do have a very small opinion of me, don't you? I can't imagine you still believe that I ran out on Ryan." Her shoulders slumped like the effort of what she was about to say took all the fight she had in her. "I left New Orleans because my in-laws told me to. They told me I had nothing to stay here for. My Ryan was dead."

"Dead? What do you mean? Are you telling me that Charles and Mamie told you Ryan was dead, so that you would leave town?"

The truth finally out, Joy felt drained. No more fights. No more taking unfair accusations. No more anything. All she wanted to do now was crawl next to Ryan and hide from everyone. She began to tremble from the burden life had become for her and sadness clouded the light in her eyes. "I meant just what I said. Charles and Mamie told me that Ryan hadn't survived the explosion and they felt it was better for me to move to L.A. and operate the store they'd given us as a wedding present. It wasn't until you called me to come back, that I found out that Ryan was alive." Joy's voice broke on the last syllable and Hank could see her small frame wracked with sobs.

In two steps he'd reached her and pulled her close to him.

"Shh...my Darling. I can't believe you didn't know. What hell you must have gone through these past years. Joy, sweetheart, can you ever forgive me? I've treated you so unfairly. You see, I thought you knew Ryan was alive, but because of his injuries, you didn't want to have anything to do with him." Hank slapped his forehead and Joy could see that he was surprised at her revelation. "God, I've been so stupid to think you, of all people, could be so insensitive. I'm truly sorry, and I'll understand if you can't forgive me." His voice sounded forlorn.

Joy could not answer. She was so tired. She stood there in the circle of his strong, yet gentle arms basking in the strength and comfort she found there, and tried to ignore the tingling sensation she felt at the proximity of his being.

Hank lowered his head and allowed his lips to gently touch down on hers. She had to admit, even to herself, his kiss was delicious and for a moment she relinquished all moral thoughts and savored the sensations it caused. Her arms crept around his neck and she entwined her fingers tightly in the curls at the nape of his neck. At this gesture of involvement, Hank deepened the kiss and prodded her lips open with his hot, searching tongue. Lost in the ecstasy of the moment, both let go of the restraints that held them bound for weeks. Hank's hands began to roam, exploring the delicious, sensuous curves of Joy's body.

Joy breathed out a gentle sigh as his hand cupped her breast. The heat from his passion was easily felt through the thin fabric of her dress as he gently pulled the dress down over her shoulders. His lips sought out the softness of her shoulders as he traced a hot trail of kisses down the side of her neck.

Joy knew in the back of her mind that they were going too far and that she should stop him but couldn't. It felt too good. She gave in to the feelings as Hank continued his search of long dreamed about places. Her dress fell to the floor and she felt the cool draft of air from the air conditioner caress her heated body. She stood there, clad only in her lace panties and bra, her breasts heaving from passion and desire. Her thick brown curls were tousled from his hand's entanglement as they kissed, her eyes were misted with desire and her lips were parted and wet.

She stood there, affirming all Hank's dreams about her. He had pictured her exactly this way so many times before and now here she stood, not in his imagination, but in all of reality.

He removed his shirt and placed Joy's hands on his chest, and she readily curled her fingers in the thick mass of hair covering the broad expanse. She could feel his muscles rippling as he slowly moved his arms to encircle her tiny waist. Her hands traveled down and came to rest on his belt buckle. She could feel his excitement thrust against her legs. His manhood was screaming to be set free from the imprisonment of his pants. She took the initiative and unbuckled his belt. The zipper slid down the track as of its own accord. The next thing Joy knew, her hands were seeking out his awakened desire.

Hank involuntarily shuddered as she grasped it, causing it to quiver. She could feel it pulsate with pent up passion and felt the dampness from his excitement.

Hank pulled her gently to the floor positioning himself over her. He held her head gently between his hands and began to tenderly rub her cheeks with his thumbs. Her cheeks were damp. Bending down to kiss her, he tasted the saltiness of tears and knew the dampness was not from passion.

"Joy? Darling, is there anything wrong?"

Not being able to speak because of the struggle going on inside her, she shook her head and began to cry, "Oh, Hank. I'm so confused. I've never felt this way before. I don't want to do this, but it's like I have no control over my body. It feels right, but Hank, we're cheating on Ryan. I do love him."

"I know you do Joy, but it's a love that can go nowhere. Darling, he can't make love to you. He'll never be able to hold you or touch you. I can Joy. Knowing Ryan, he'd give us his blessing. I know he would. He once promised me, he'd love you for the both of us and circumstances caused him to break that promise. I make that promise now, I'll love you for the both of us."

"It doesn't work that way, Hank. I'm still married to Ryan and I will be faithful to him until death takes him away from me."

Hurt and humiliated by Joy's rebuttal, Hank retorted, "Were you faithful to him with Shaze? Or did your belief in Ryan's death allow you to make love to him?" Seeing the hurt look in her face he cried, "dammit, Joy, I've loved you since high school. I've never been able to love anyone else." His voice held all the anguish he'd kept bottled up for the better part of his life.

Angry with herself for messing up Hank's life and betraying her wedding vows to Ryan, Joy spat out, "Well, Hank, what can I say? I'm a bitch. Yeah, that's it! I'm a bitch with a capital "B". What do you want me to do? Sleep with you to satisfy our lustful desires? Ryan may not be able to make love to me physically, but dammit, he makes love to me every time he looks at me or smiles at me. I feel it! Yes, damn you; I feel it in every fiber of my being. You may not feel that we've done anything wrong, but I do." Striking her breast with her fist, she repeated, "I do." Sobbing openly now, Joy glared at Hank.

He stood there fuming at the pain and guilt she was putting herself through, and knowing that he'd added to it made him even more furious. He could see in her eyes what she could not or would not let herself admit to, she loved him. Yes, she was torn in two, but her guilt at loving him was really what was tormenting her.

Not being able to stand it any longer, Hank grabbed his shirt, and stomped to the door. Joy seemed oblivious to the fact that he was leaving, so lost was she in her sobs and her guilt. He shook his head, whispered, "I love you," and walked out of the house.

She sat there in the darkened house, in the early morning hours and tried to make sense of her life, wondering for just the briefest of moments, if she would not have been better off refusing to come back to New Orleans.

# CHAPTER 11

She met Hank the next day at the hospital and her turmoil was evident in her swollen, darkly circled eyes. Hank, too, looked like he'd visited hell and was kicked back to reality. Their response to each other was stilted and reserved. Hank visited with Ryan long enough to let him know he was there and excused himself saying he had the beginnings of a sore throat and didn't want to take the risk of passing it on to him.

Joy sat at Ryan's bedside and told him of her plans to go to L.A. in a few days to take care of selling the L.A. store. It caused her so much pain to look into his eyes and see the fear her leaving caused him.

"I know Sweetheart, I hate the idea of leaving, but you know I've been away for so long and decisions need to be made. I thought I'd put the store up for sale. Remember? We talked about it last week. I need to put my house up for sale and see about moving all my belongings here. And there's my cat, Patches. Oh, love, I wish you could meet her. She's the most delightful little creature. She showed up on my front stoop one day and was suffering from starvation and neglect. I took her in and fed her and she just took to me like she'd been waiting for me all her life."

Ryan looked at Joy and attempted a feeble smile and whispered, "I know what you mean," and Joy knew he was thinking of how he had taken to her, as though he'd waited a lifetime for her too.

Patting his hand, she continued. She knew she was babbling on but was so nervous about his reaction to her leaving she couldn't stop herself. "Anyway, she's the prettiest little cat now. I know you would love her. She's a calico and has the best personality in the world. Anyway, I need to bring her home too. You see love, there's so much to do." Exhaling a long breath, she squeezed his hand, "but if you really don't want me to go, I'll wait."

Ryan looked at her with his one good eye and Joy watched as a tear fell from his eye and trickled down his cheek. She bent over, kissed the tear away, and heard him say, "Go love, do what you have to and hurry home, please." Pausing to take another breath, he added, "we need you." She noticed how hard it was for him to say just these few words. His health was declining rapidly and she found herself sometimes thinking that maybe it would be better if his heart failed. The struggle he was going through to stay alive was unbelievable. Often she wondered if it was truly worth the struggle, because each day he lived, his pain increased. Though he never complained about the pain, she knew it was there. In a crazy sort of way, she felt it right along with him.

Ryan, exhausted, fell asleep and Joy sat in the chair next to his bedside, holding his hand and softly singing to him. The room gradually grew darker but neither of them noticed.

Later that afternoon, Hank returned to the room to find Joy sleeping in the chair next to Ryan's bed, still holding his hand. Walking over to her, he placed a soft kiss on the top of her head.

Startled, she sprang from her chair. She could see Hank in the dimly lit room, holding a finger over his lips in a gesture of silence. Noticing the darkness of the room for the first time, she reached over and switched on the lamp next to the bed. Looking down at Ryan, she gasped.

His face was deeply flushed and shiny with perspiration. Joy reached out her hand and felt his damp clothing. She touched his face and found it to be feverish. She saw his chest heaving as he fought a losing battle with the deep rattle that was robbing him of his breath.

Alarmed, she looked over at Hank. Motioning her to the door, he grabbed her shoulders and told her he thought the doctor should be summoned. As her hot tears coursed down her cheeks, she silently nodded in agreement.

In no matter of time, Hank returned with the doctor. Without a glance in Joy's direction, the doctor hurried to Ryan's bedside and began to examine him. Joy could only watch and wring her hands in consternation as the doctor preformed his task. Examination complete, the doctor looked at Joy and gestured her to follow him into the hallway. Helpless, Joy followed him.

Softly closing the door behind them, the doctor turned sorrowful eyes on Joy. She could feel the fear of what he was going to tell her build up inside her. Before he could utter a word, Joy spun on him, "No, uh uh no way. You are not going to tell me there is nothing you can do for him. I won't accept it. Do you hear me? Ryan is not going to die! I won't let him." Her words were coming out forcefully at first, then sobs took over and drowned them. The doctor watched as her body shivered with agony.

"Joy, I know this is hard for you, but I'm afraid my news is not good. Ryan's body is full of infection and now pneumonia has taken over both of his lungs. His fever is up and his blood pressure is much too high." The doctor sucked in his breath. This was always so hard. Especially when he was as close to a patient as he was to Ryan. He placed his hands on Joy's shoulders, "what I'm about to say to you is said as a friend, not as a physician. Do you understand?"

Joy shook her head indicating she did.

"Good," the doctor continued, "perhaps Ryan's death would be more of a blessing than life itself."

Joy's head shot up as she glared at the man. He held his hand up in a gesture indicating she should wait for him to finish, then he continued, "I know you just found each other again, but Joy, holding on to him like this is no good for either of you. Be strong." Increasing his grip on her shoulders, he looked into her eyes, "let him go. God knows, the man deserves his rest."

Pain ravaged Joy's soul as she returned the doctor's look. Her determination to hold on to Ryan was slipping as his words sank into her mind. The weight of his words ladened with truth caused her shoulders to sag as though the weight of the world was positioned there. In a voice broken with despair, she thanked the doctor for his advice.

"I'll try but, God, I love him so much. It's so unfair. Why? Why did all of this happen to us?" Joy didn't expect an answer from the doctor and he knew it.

He placed his arms around her and gave her a hug. "Good girl, now please go home and get some rest. We'll call you if anything changes. You know you might get called back in the middle of the night and you would be more help to us if you were rested. You would be no help to us or to Ryan if you were dead on your feet."

"Not yet, I need more time with him, you understand don't you? I'll go home and get some rest, but not now." Joy turned from the doctor and went back into the room where her beloved was slipping away from her. She did not see the tears spill from the doctor's eyes as he turned his back to the door and walked away filled with fatigue and helplessness.

Inside Ryan's room, Hank pulled a chair next to Joy's and took her hand in his. They sat and waited at Ryan's bedside. Neither said a word and both were lost in their thoughts as they watched him struggle to breathe.

"Joy." The sound was barely audible but was enough to bring her out of her thoughts. She looked around then looked at Hank to see if he had heard it too. He just sat there, still lost in his thoughts. Hank had not heard it and in truth, it was but a sound uttered on a sigh.

Joy sprang to her husband's side. Taking his feverish hand in hers, she whispered words that she hoped would bring him comfort. Time was running out and she did not know when he would stop hearing her tell him of her love for him.

"Ryan, my beloved husband," she whispered, "if I could put into words my love for you, they would be the most beautiful song ever written. I love you, my darling. There has never been another one to take your place. I don't think there will ever be anyone I'll love like I love you." She tried to hold back her tears but the task was too hard. They spilled from her eyes, making gentle splatters on Ryan's feverish skin, as she gently caressed him with her words of love.

Hank, creeping up quietly behind Joy, heard her make this confession to her husband. It was as though a searing hot knife was shoved into his chest causing such pain, as he had never felt before in his life. Quietly, he turned and walked away from the two people he loved most in this world. The pain tearing through his chest was a combination of sorrow at the imminent loss of his friend, that had been more of a brother to him, and the loss of the only woman he ever loved. He stood by the window gazing out at the early evening twilight, not seeing the glimmer of stars in the softly darkening sky. His tears blinded him to everything but his plight.

Glancing behind her, Joy saw Hank standing by the window, his shoulders shaking with the burden of his tears. She wanted to go to him, to comfort him as he had comforted her so many times in the last few days, but couldn't bear to leave Ryan's side, even for a minute. Turning back to Ryan, she read his dry, cracked lips as he feebly called out for his lifetime buddy.

"Hank," she called out softly. Hank turned from the window. "Ryan's calling for you," she said as she waved him to the bed.

In two steps he was by his friend's bedside. He picked up Ryan's hand, noticing at once the heat emanating from it. "Here I am, good buddy. What can I do for you, pal?" Hank's voice was breaking and Joy noticed that he wasn't trying to conceal it this time.

Ryan lay there, looking at the two people he loved most in this world. Tears ran down his fevered cheek making a trail down to his chin. Joy reached over to wipe his face but he shook his head. Joy withdrew her hand.

"No fights. No more."

Hank and Joy looked at each other. Ryan knew of their fights! Joy shook her head at Hank's unasked question. "No, I haven't told him of our fights, have you?" Hank echoed her answer. Then it came to them. Of course he'd known. After all, he was a part of the trio too, wasn't he? He'd felt their hostility all along. He'd known, and had never brought it up. They hung their heads in shame as they each reprimanded themselves for their behavior.

In an unexpected burst of strength, Ryan reached out, caught Joy's hand, and lifted it. He placed it over his heart allowing her to feel his weakened heartbeat. His gaze never left her face as he reached out and grabbed Hank's hand. With all the strength he could muster, he brought Hank's hand up to cover hers. He had to get his message to them, no matter the cost. He knew his time was running out. The tears ran unchecked, spilling down his scarred cheeks. Feebly he squeezed their hands and uttered one word, "love," then closed his eyes.

Hank and Joy held their breath as they waited to see if the next breath would come. Finally and thankfully, they saw him exhale ever so lightly.

Hank too exhaled, "don't worry, good buddy. I'll take care of everything," he whispered.

Ryan slowly opened his eye again. He looked at the two of them, attempted a smile then drifted back into a semi-conscious state.

Blinded by her tears and her grief, Joy was not aware of her hand being covered by Hank's until she felt a tightening grip that caused enough pain to bring her back to the present. Her head jerked up, wondering why her hand was being gripped so hard, and found Hank a broken man. She had never seen a man cry so openly and so hard as she now saw him cry. His tears brought her out of her selfish pain as she thought of the pain Ryan's best friend was going through.

He was so lost in his pain, he never noticed her slipping her hand from his grasp. She walked to him and placed her arms around him, hoping to give him some comfort, but Hank being the man he was, ended up comforting her as the two of them stood next to the bed of their partner and sobbed, not for him so much as for themselves and the final loss they would experience when he left them.

Ryan died later that evening with both of his friends by his bedside. Hank held his hand and Joy placed a last kiss on his dry parched lips. He'd opened his eye, looked at the two of them and repeated his plea of before, this time followed by another word, "promise." He closed his eyes, never to open them again.

Numb, Joy turned from the bed and walked out of the room.

Ryan was buried alongside his mother and father two days later following a very small and private burial service. After the funeral, Joy and Hank sat under one of the giant oak trees bordering the cemetery. Neither wanted to leave. Leaving would make it all so final. So they sat there reminiscing about the antics of the trio. They talked about everything except for the one thing uppermost in both of their minds. Ryan's last request. They knew in their hearts what he meant, but neither voiced it.

While Joy thought they had time for that, Hank was afraid to bring it up, fearful of pushing her too soon. Yet, he feared now that Ryan was gone; she would turn again to Shaze. So, it was with dread that he took the news a couple of days after the funeral that she was leaving town. She broke this news to him over the phone informing him she was leaving within the hour. This gave him no time to discuss anything with her and that infuriated him. He feared he'd lost her again. This time for good.

Joy on the other hand, arranged this so that she could have time to sort out her thoughts and her feelings. Things were bad enough with her having to confront Shaze after all this time, without Hank pressuring her about decisions she needed to make. Her return trip was dreary. The flight was uneventful and was spent in quiet meditation.

Joy tried to relax and enjoy the flight knowing that once she arrived and faced Shaze, all hell would break loose. She did not call ahead to say she was coming in. Her thoughts were troubled as she drove the rental to the suburbs and to the much-missed little cottage she called home. It was dusk as she pulled into her driveway.

The early evening breeze was cool and the stars were starting to peek out of their daytime hiding places. The smell of roses from her rose garden wafted gently to her as she stood in front of her own little house, so unlike the one she now owned in New Orleans. All prim and proper with its little window boxes filled with a colorful array of blooming flowers.

How uncomplicated my life was when I last left this, she thought, but then I only thought Ryan was dead. Now I know he's dead. Her heart weighed heavy with the thoughts of Ryan and all their lost years.

Now as she took in the sight of her cottage on the hill, she realized the immensity of her decisions. Would she stay here and forget New Orleans and everyone in it. Would she sell what she owned in New Orleans or would she sell her things here in Los Angeles? Would she marry Shaze as planned, or would she break that off and hope for a future with Hank? Confused, she shrugged her shoulders as though to leave her problems at the door, and let herself into the cool tranquility of her house.

The look of fear on Beth's face at the sound of someone in the foyer was soon replaced by delight as she jumped up with a squeal and hugged her friend.

"What are you doing here? Why haven't you come home before? Never mind, you're here now and it's about time. Do you realize how much I've missed you? Poor Patches, she thinks her mistress has died. She goes around the house looking confused." Beth just kept rambling on. When she finally shut up, she took a good look at Joy, took in a sharp breath then let out a slow whistle. "Girl, what in the world happened to you? You look like hell warmed over."

Beth had always been a little envious of Joy's good looks but now felt pity for the woman that stood before her. She was not exaggerating when she said that Joy looked like hell warmed over. Joy had always possessed an air of certainty and had always carried herself well, giving an impression of someone who knew who they were. Now, she stood there, shoulders slumped as though they carried the weight of the world on them. Her magnificent hair, the cause of most of Beth's envy, now looked dull and lifeless. Her stylish clothes hung on her diminished frame. But, the most drastic change of all was in Joy's eyes. Once they were the outstanding features on Joy's beautiful face, sad and liquid looking, giving one the impression she was on the verge of tears, but always tender and friendly. Now they looked dismal. Hauntingly sad. They no longer had brilliance, they were dark and dull. They stood out in her thin face like large beacons of misery. The once composed face was now a mask of confusion and sorrow. So unlike the Joy that Beth knew.

Exhausted after all that had happened, Joy allowed herself to fall heavily in a chair, kicked off her shoes and said, "friend, I'll tell you all if you would just be nice enough to fix me a drink. Make it a stiff one."

Another change. Joy had been known to drink now and then but she'd never had a "stiff one" before.

Anxious at the prospect of finding out what had happened to Joy to cause all these changes in her, Beth jumped up and fixed a drink for the two of them. Even though her curiosity was at an all time high she decided to give Joy a little time before making her go into what had evidently been an ordeal for her. So as they sat and nursed their drinks, Beth filled Joy in on the store business. When she finished with that, Joy asked her about Shaze. Slapping her forehead, Beth replied, "Shaze? Oh, gosh…, you're here! Man will he ever be pissed."

"Beth, for Pete's sake, please stop your rambling and tell me what do you mean? Is Shaze here? Was he expecting me?"

"Joy," Beth began to laugh at the irony of it all, "Shaze left tonight for New Orleans. He said he had enough of this quote, damn waiting, unquote and he wasn't going to wait any longer. He's probably in New Orleans now."

Joy looked at Beth, "damn, girl, this is not funny," then she began to laugh also. It seemed ages since she'd laughed and gave over to the sensation, but her laughter was on the verge of hysteria. The two women sat there, rolling in laughter, then sobering up Beth looked intensely at Joy. She stretched out her hand and touched Joy's arm, "let's be serious now, Joy. I know this is not a funny matter. Shaze was in one hell of a strange mood, girlfriend."

"A strange mood? What do you mean, Beth?"

"Joy, I can't prove anything, but I think he's in some sort of trouble. He's been acting weird lately. At times, he seems lost and distracted and other times he's in a vile mood. He walks around like a firecracker about to explode. He really frightens me. I know you don't like me to say things like that about him, but Joy, it's true. He frightens the hell out of me and I'll tell you something else," she shook her head for emphasis, "I think he's on drugs." Afraid that she'd said too much she added, "crap, let's change the subject, just talking about him gives me the creeps." As an afterthought, Beth looked at Joy, "just be careful when you're with him Joy, I think he's changed and I don't think you should trust him." Beth shivered and Joy saw her wrap her arms around herself as if to reassure herself she was safe.

The lump in Joy's stomach turned to lead and she felt a tremor of fear run through her at the thought of facing him. She remembered very well, his behavior in New Orleans and how she thought back then that he'd changed. Beth, without knowing it, had just confirmed Joy's worst fears.

"Well, I guess I need to find out where he is and tell him to stay put. If he finds out I'm not in New Orleans and has to fly back here, I'm sure he will be pissed." Before she lost nerve, she called the hotel to see if Shaze was registered. She was informed he had made a reservation but would not be there until the next day.

"Great, fantastic, just what I need." Her voice was brittle as she hung the phone up. Facing Beth she said. "I'm finally ready to face him and he's not here, he's not in New Orleans, he's somewhere between here and there and now I'll have another night to worry about."

At the look of exasperation on her face Beth tried to lighten the moment. "Look at the positive side of this Joy, at least it will give you a few more hours to get yourself together before you have to talk to him. Besides, you look too tired to travel tonight. Even if Shaze had made it to New Orleans tonight, you would not have been able to go to him right away. And I know you want to talk to him but, frankly Joy, I don't think you're up to it." Beth had no idea what Joy wanted to talk to Shaze about, and from the look on her face, she felt sure it was not to finalize the wedding plans.

Joy smiled at her friend who had for the last few months, lived in her house, ran her businesses and had taken care of her cat for her. "You're right and you're wrong. I am too tired for any type of travel tonight and truthfully, I don't want to talk to Shaze. I don't want to, but I have to." She looked at the cute little spitfire that she considered her best friend. "I promised you I'd tell you everything and I have a lot to tell you, but first, I want a hot bath, then we'll talk, okay?"

Beth, hungry for the companionship the two had shared before the phone call from New Orleans had disrupted their lives, pushed Joy into the bathroom and laughingly told her to hurry. She had waited too long already and her curiosity was at its peak.

# CHAPTER 12

*A*n hour later, Joy emerged from the bathroom refreshed and smiling. While in the tub she had taken inventory of the choices her life offered her and she had to concede they weren't bad. She was now a millionaire a few times over, she owned a number of jewelry stores that were doing exceedingly well and although she had to say a final goodbye to Ryan, she had found Hank.

Joy had promised herself the day of the funeral that she would say goodbye to her beloved and not hold on to a love that could never be fulfilled. For her well being and for Ryan's peace she had decided to go forward with her life.

While relaxing in the tub, she had finally allowed herself to think of Hank and her feelings for him. Somewhere deep inside her, she knew she'd loved him all along. It was just that her love for Ryan had overshadowed everything else. She'd loved them both, but her love for Ryan had been stronger than her love for Hank. This love now seemed to burst forward in a surge of strong liberation. It seemed as though it was screaming, at last, finally, I'm free to grow.

Beth noticed the change in Joy as she came from the bathroom. Smiling at her friend, she beckoned her to sit as she placed a tray of sandwiches on the coffee table in front of them.

Joy sat curled up with her feet under her body and munching on a sandwich, she began to tell Beth the story of everything that had happened before her wedding and then she told her of everything that had happened since. The only thing she didn't tell Beth was Shaze's behavior while in New Orleans.

Beth cried with Joy at parts of the story and laughed with her as she shared some of the fun things she, Ryan and Hank had done together so long ago. She was awed at the fact that her friend was now so independently wealthy, but was so happy for her. She had known that Joy'd had a rough life as a child and it restored her faith in life to see that someone so deserving had been rewarded, although she fully realized that to receive that reward, Joy had to suffer hell and she was sure that the woman sitting in front of her would have chosen life with Ryan instead of all this wealth, had the choice been given her. But now she had this other guy, Hank. She had noticed the glimmer of light shine in the dull eyes of her boss and friend as she said his name, but just as quick as the light shone, it was diminished. Beth knew Joy was battling with guilt and she swore to herself that she would do whatever she had to, to get Joy to acknowledge the fact that she loved Hank.

"Hey girlfriend, I think you're holding out on me. Come clean girlie, fess up." Beth reached over and playfully slapped Joy on the arm.

"What are you talking about, nosey? I've told you everything. What do you mean, I'm holding out on you?"

"Hey, do I dare hope there's a new man in your life? One that makes your eyes light up like stars at the mere mention of his name." Beth noticed a deep blush cover Joy's flawless cheeks as she softened her tone and grew serious. "I've never seen you look so lovely, Joy as when you speak about Hank. You really love him don't you? You know, you never looked like that when you talked about Shaze." The words were barely out of her mouth when she had to duck a flying pillow aimed straight at her.

"Yes, nose trouble, I do love Hank. I know this will sound crazy, but I've always loved him. Even while I loved Ryan, I loved Hank."

Joy let herself bask in the warmth her words created. "I love Hank and Ryan knew it." Her eyes grew pensive and Beth could see tears threatening to spill over. In a soft hushed voice she said, "Beth, before he died, Ryan placed my hand over his heart and took Hank's hand and covered mine. He looked at the two of us and said love. Later, just before he died, he said it again this time adding promise. It was like he was giving us his blessing or more like giving us to each other."

Beth sat there utterly amazed. "Wow" was all she could say; as she reflected on the tightly knit relationship the three of them had shared.

Joy caught Beth's hand between the two of hers and looking at her she agreed, "you're right, Beth. I've never felt this way with Shaze. I'm afraid to think of the mistake I would've made if Charles hadn't requested me to return to New Orleans. God, I would have married Shaze. I don't know what I was thinking when I committed myself to him. I thought I loved him but I see now that that was not love. The man just has some sort of magnetism about him that just seems to draw me to him. I wish I could explain it. That's what scares me. He has this effect on me that destroys my sensibility." Seeing the worried look on Beth's face she hurriedly added, "but I'll be strong. Somehow I will break it off with him."

Beth's eyes met Joy's and a look was exchanged between the two women that conveyed fear and foreboding. They said no more that night about Shaze. They turned instead to going over the things that Joy had to take care of.

"What are you going to do about the stores, Joy? How are you going to take care of them now that you have all the other stores to be concerned about?" Beth's voice was strained and she fidgeted as she waited for the reply.

"I suppose I'll handle it the way I'll handle all the others. You know Charles was seldom in the stores after a while. He had general managers that ran everything for him. I've met two of the managers and I'm quite impressed by them. It seems they've been with Charles for ten years and have no intentions of leaving. I've made sure of that." She cast a sidelong glance at Beth and smiled inwardly at the worry etched on her friend's face.

"Did you arrange for one of the general managers to take over your stores or are you going to look for someone else?" Her voice hesitated as she thought of working for someone other than Joy.

"I've already found my general manager for the L.A. store and I don't mind telling you that with the salary I'll be paying her, she'll be happy here." The pent up laughter was beginning to smother her as she saw Beth's face fall then turn a deep shade of red. "What about you Beth, you are planning on staying on aren't you?"

Beth couldn't look at Joy. She was dangerously close to tears and she didn't want Joy to feel guilty about it. She would just find another place to work. "Uh, Joy I've been thinking about leaving L.A. The only reason I've stayed is because of you. Maybe I'll move to New Orleans with you. Do you think there might be a spot for me in one of Charles's stores?"

Joy did not expect this answer. She always thought Beth loved it here in L.A. Her hand shot out, grabbing Beth's hands as the tears spilled over and fell to Beth's cheeks. "Beth, are you serious? Do you dislike Los Angeles?"

"No Joy, I love it here. But I don't think I like the idea of working for someone else. I don't know if I want to work for a stranger." Her voice trembled as she confided in Joy. She was like a terrified child.

"Big silly," Joy told her as she began to giggle, "you would still be working for me. I still own the store and I promise you'll get along fine with my new general manager. You'll love her just the way I do. As a matter of fact, she's not a stranger at all."

"Not-a-stranger? Do I know her, Joy?"

"I sure hope you know her. Would you like to meet her?" Joy reached over and pulled a compact out of her purse. She opened it and handed the case to Beth. "Beth, I would like you to meet my new general manager for the L.A. operations."

Beth gazed back at her reflection in the compact mirror. Her emerald green eyes grew large as she looked at her reflected image then at Joy. "What do you mean? Am I...oh no, you can't mean me. You want me as your new general manager?" Her voice was filled with disbelief.

Joy held her breath as she shook her head yes. "Beth you are the only one I would ever trust to run that store. If you tell me no, I'll sell it. Honest! And you know what that store means to me. Truthfully, for a while I thought about selling it, but now that Ryan is dead, well, truth be known, I can't sell it. It was a wedding gift and I just can't part with it right now. Please don't make me sell it. I know you love this city and the store. If you accept, then I would expect you to over-see the Shreveport store also. I know you fell in love with that part of Louisiana when you came with me to check on things there. I would expect you to fly there once or twice a month and I thought maybe you'd like the change of scenery. But if you don't want the responsi-bility of both stores, maybe I could sell the Louisiana store. The L.A. store is so much bigger and..."

"Wh...what did you say that new salary was?" Beth threw her arms around Joy and hugged her tightly. "You are an amazing woman Joy Young. I would be delighted and honored to be you gen-eral manager for the L.A. store and your Louisiana store. You won't be needing to sell anything girlfriend. I'll take the whole bag."

Joy hugged her back, "there's only one stipulation Beth."

Beth's joy began to fade as she thought Joy would ask her to keep Shaze on the payroll. Taking a deep breath, she steeled herself to put up a fight if she had to, for she had already decided firing Shaze would be her first official act as general manager. "What is it, Joy?"

"You have to promise me never to let our employees see you with that red runny nose." She rolled out of the way just in time to avoid being pummeled by a shrieking Beth.

The problem of the store finished she went on to the problem of the house. But this was quickly taken care of when she found out that Beth had grown attached to it and wanted to buy it. They settled on a fair price only after Beth cajoled Joy into throwing Patches in with the house. Beth, elated and not believing all that had just transpired spent the rest of the night thinking about the generosity of the woman in the next room.

Joy was up early the next morning anxious to get the day started so she could get on with her life. She phoned the hotel again, and this time was told the reservation in Shaze's name was confirmed for an afternoon arrival. She left a message for him saying that she had flown back from New Orleans to see him and had missed him. She told him to stay there, that she was returning later that day and she would meet him at the hotel.

Beth bade her goodbye with hugs and tears before leaving to open the store. Joy packed the clothes she needed, Beth was going to ship the rest of her things to her later, took a last look around and walked out of the house.

As Joy flew over one side of the country to the other, the only thing that marred her happiness was the task at hand. The one she had to face as soon as she arrived in New Orleans. God, please be with me, she silently asked the One unseen. She closed her eyes and conjured images of Hank hoping they would dispel the fear she felt at the aspect of telling Shaze goodbye forever. She tried to reassure herself that she had nothing to be afraid of; that Shaze loved her too much to harm her but found it offered little comfort. Fear was set in every filament of her being, invoking terrible images caused by an infuriated Shaze. Her thoughts of Hank would dispel the horrible images for a while but then thoughts of Shaze would invade her mind again chasing the comforting thoughts away.

The flight was much too short and much too soon Joy found herself in the lobby of Le Pavillon. Choosing to face this head-on she walked to the desk and asked for Shaze's room number. Taking a deep breath she entered the elevator.

# CHAPTER 13

She looked more assured than she felt. Now that the time to face Shaze was actually here, her confidence was waning. She was grateful she hadn't told him the exact time of her arrival. If he'd known her arrival time he would've been waiting for her and as much as she wanted it over with, she just wasn't ready to face him.

Joy raised her hand to knock on the door at the same time the door swung open. There he stood, in his khaki slacks and white polo shirt. Joy took in a sharp breath as she stood and looked at the man she had promised to marry. It was no wonder she'd told him yes. He was a man few women could resist.

His attractiveness was striking. His dark features and sleepy looking brown eyes surrounded him in a mysterious ambiance. His eyes, so dark brown they were almost black, acted as magnets pulling at anything they looked at. It was his eyes and smile, showing strong straight teeth and ending in dimples deep enough to put the tip of a finger in, that had gotten Joy in trouble the first time she'd seen him. He only had to look at any woman and smile and her heart was instantly his, and she had been no exception. His thick dark hair worn pulled back into a neat small ponytail, didn't hurt his looks either. He looked like a model just stepping out of a fashionable men's magazine. Facing him now Joy felt her heart quiver. The magnetic gaze was pulling at her heartstrings again and she knew she would have to resist, and it wasn't going to be easy. The man's smile could melt anyone's heart.

Except Beth's, thought Joy, as she remembered Beth's warning. And Beth was right. She couldn't trust him, no matter how good looking he was. She forced herself to imagine Hank by her side. Please dear Lord, she pleaded, let me be strong and do what I have to do.

"Joy, my darling." The surprised look on Shaze's face told Joy he wasn't expecting her. "My God, it's been so long." Shaze pulled her close to him affording her a hefty scent of his spicy cologne. "Oh, baby, let me just look at you. God, I've dreamed of you every night since we've been apart. I've dreamed of holding you like this. Please, Joy, please, never take your love from me. I don't know what I'd do. I need you so damn much." He gently pushed her away from him to get a better look at her and then pulled her tighter against him as he rambled on and the only thing Joy really heard, was his plea for her to never take her love from him.

Laughing to hide her nervousness, Joy hugged Shaze lightly and pulled away from him. "Shaze, it's good to see you too. Weren't you expecting me? I left a message at the front desk for you, telling you I was coming. Didn't you get it?"

A sheepish grin covered Shaze's face. "I didn't check with the desk for messages. I arrived here just a short while ago and didn't expect any messages." And then as reality set in, he gave her a quizzical look. "Uh, how did you know I was here?"

Joy evaded his question. "You seem to be going out, I can come back if you have some place to go, Shaze." She knew he was obviously lying to her about his arrival. According to the information she'd received this morning, he should have been here for a few hours by now. Funny how easily I catch him in lies now, she thought. Joy wondered how many lies he'd told her in the past, when she'd had no reason to doubt him.

"Don't be silly. Now that you're here, where would I go? I was on my way to your house. And now that you're here, all I want is to take you in my arms and love you. It's been so damn long," he repeated. Now that she actually was with him he was not about to let her go and he prayed that his charm still worked on her. He had lied to her about just arriving and the notion of her knowing he was here made him a little nervous.

Joy gave no noticeable sign indicating she knew about his lie. She knew she would have to put on an act worthy of an Academy award, so she pasted a smile on her face and relaxed her voice. "I know. It has been a long time and I'm sorry, but things just kept happening that prevented me from leaving and then when I finally got a chance to go, you would know it, you had come back here. It seemed like we would never connect, didn't it? But, hey, I'm here, you're here, I guess we're connecting, huh?" She prayed Shaze would pick up on the joking that she desperately was trying to start. To her way of thinking, if she could keep him in a light and joking mood, things would go better for her.

"You went back to L.A. to see me?" He let out a hidden sigh of relief, so that's how she knew he was here. The bitch Beth, probably told her he'd come here to see her. Grateful she was in a playful mood he picked up on her banter, "hey, baby, if it's connecting you want, I sure can take care of that, in a New York minute." He lunged for her from across the sofa. She jumped back from his grasp. Shaze jumped from the sofa and feigned a chase around the room in pursuit of Joy.

Exhausted from her trips to and from L.A. and the stress of having to break her relationship with him had Joy in a mood that definitely was not actively playful. "C'mon Shaze, look, let's go out. It's such a beautiful day today; Let's go out to the French Market. I've been craving beignets and café a lait. It's been years since I've gone to Café Du Monde. Let's go, please. It'll be so much fun. You know it's been years since I've been through the Quarter." The desperation and longing in her voice took the desired effect on Shaze.

Joy sensed it and before he could say or do anything, she had pulled the door open and stepped out into the hallway. Seeing there was nothing he could do to stop her and thinking that there was plenty of time to be alone later, Shaze pulled his jacket off the back of the chair and followed her into the busy streets of New Orleans.

The streets were teeming with people as they always were in this older part of the city. It was such a beautiful day, Joy convinced Shaze that walking the few blocks to the French Quarter would do them both good. The French Quarter throbbed with a heartbeat of its own and it showed in the merriment surrounding them. New Orleans seemed to have the same effect on other people as it had on Joy, as she pushed aside all unpleasant thoughts and gave in to the delicious excitement around her.

They strolled through the French Quarter stopping shortly at a few of the many shops along Bourbon Street. Although still early, jazz musicians could be heard from the open doorways of some of the clubs. Looking around, Joy saw the ever-present street kids dancing for the spectators, while hoping to make a few dollars. Managers of clubs stood in open doorways, enticing the teeming visitors to take advantage of the cool dim interiors of their establishments, promising exotic surprises to those who gave in. Novelty shops abounded, advertising their wares in the storefront windows, some of which caused Joy to blush with embarrassment.

And the visitors loved it all. They shouted in excited tones at each other from across the street and it seemed no one there was a stranger.

The crowds grew a little thinner as Joy and Shaze made their way to Jackson Square. Joy felt the tingle of anticipation, for this was one of her favorite spots in the entire city. Trying to subdue the rising memories of the many Saturdays and Sundays spent strolling through the Square with Ryan and Hank, Joy chatted about everything she saw. The Square, she told Shaze, was once used as a parade ground for colonial troops and was given the name Jackson Square in 1851 when General Andrew Jackson became the hero of the Battle of New Orleans. She pointed out the statue of the general who occupies the center of the square. The statue, she commented, is still regal and strong. "Can you imagine, Shaze, being such a hero that a statue is erected of you and given a place of honor like this?" Shaze didn't respond. Joy kept walking and taking in the sights she'd pushed to the rear of her memory so long ago. Artists still hung their wares on the iron fence surrounding Jackson Square and were as always, sitting in front of their easels. Some were sketching the magnificent St. Louis Cathedral, which faces the square, others with fingers smudged with charcoal or pastels, diligently drew the likeness of the people posing for them and others still, sat, reading and waiting patiently for their next customer. Interspersed among the artists sat the tarot readers, pondering their cards and predicting the future for those who paid. It was one of these that jolted Joy back to the present.

Going through the Square to the French Market, Joy noticed one reader in particular. A slender woman with long gray hair pulled away from her face in a sleek tail at the nape of her neck, wearing a brilliant orange and gold ankle length skirt with a gold top. Colorful beads hung around the woman's neck and bracelets of silver ran up her arm.

She had looked at Joy; not bothering to return the smile offered her. Joy, in turn, brushed it off as characteristic for the eccentric looking woman. But changed her mind as on the way back through the Square, the same woman caught Joy's hand and in a hoarse throaty voice, vehemently whispered, "you are in danger," then released her hand. It was all done in a matter of seconds and Shaze never noticed it happened.

Shaken by the woman's bizarre behavior, Joy grew pensive.

Noticing that Joy had suddenly grown quiet, Shaze took her hand in his and shook it as to loosen her up. "What's wrong, city girl, are you getting tired?"

Snapped out of her thoughts she tried to regain her jovial mood, "no, not tired, but I am getting thirsty. Let's go to Pat O'Brien's.

"What about the Market and Café Du Monde? Have you changed your mind about the beignets? Just think about those sweet little fried breads covered in powdered sugar. Umm, it makes my mouth water just thinking about them."

Joy shook her head. "Yes, I've changed my mind, Shaze. I think I want to go to Pat's instead. It will be cool in the courtyard and I would like one of their tall cool drinks."

Smiling, he took her elbow and guided her through the hazy streets back into the French Quarter and in to Pat O'Brien's. The patio lounge was just as enchanting as it had always been.

She remembered graduation night when she, Ryan, Hank and a group of their classmates had tried to get in. They had almost succeeded. Their failure to convince the door manager of their "legal age" hadn't thwarted Joy's excitement, for she had gotten what she wanted. She had been inside the doors long enough to see the interior. It had been the most romantic place she'd ever seen. The area had been covered with large exotic plants and trees filled with small glittering lights, had helped the star studded sky above, shine down on the lovers as they swayed in the gentle night breeze to the soft romantic music being played by the dreamy eyed women sitting at the twin pianos flanking the door. The smell of gardenias mixed in with the heady perfumes of the elegantly dressed women had hung in the air like a cloud. Ryan had promised to bring her back there and dance with her under the stars, but time had run out for them.

She and Shaze found a table near the fountain in the rear of the courtyard. Shaze ordered Pat O'Brien's famous Hurricanes for both of them, despite Joy's pleas for something less potent.

"Relax, enjoy," he prompted. "I think we should celebrate. After all these weeks, we're finally together and we have a lot to catch up on. I promise, if I see you losing control, I'll take the drink away from you."

Joy, afraid to ruin his good mood forced out a laugh and gave in.

The atmosphere surrounding her finally took effect and she began to slowly relax. Looking around her, she let out a sigh, "God, I didn't realize how much I missed this city. I'd forgotten how the excitement here gets into your blood and flows through your veins. I suppose the old saying is true—you can take the Cajun out of New Orleans, but you can't take New Orleans out of the Cajun."

Shaze took a long swallow of his drink and shook his head in agreement, "I know what you mean. I've always loved this city, although I never really was able to take advantage of the things it had to offer. You know, though I lived here…"

Joy's head snapped up. "You lived here? I thought you said you lived near New Orleans."

Joy watched as Shaze's eyes darkened and the tanned coloring of his face turned from slightly brown to deep bronze as he sputtered, "Uh, that's what I meant. I lived near enough to New Orleans to say that I lived in New Orleans. When I told people where I was from, they acted as though they'd never heard of the place, so instead of explaining to them, I just took the easy way out and said I was from New Orleans."

"Oh," said Joy as she watched him nervously finger his glass.

Damn, he'd slipped again. He wondered if she bought that story. Joy was much too smart and sometimes just being with her taxed him to the brink of his limits. Being so close to achieving the goal of his lifetime, he knew he had to be careful and could not afford slip-ups like this one. He felt like he had to be constantly on guard with his actions and his words.

"Shaze, Shaze….earth to Shaze…come in Shaze…"

He came out of his thoughts to the sound of Joy calling his name and waving her hand in front of his eyes. "Huh? What…"

"Shaze, I was asking you if you could show me where you were brought up. I really would like to see it, someday." Surprised by her own words, Joy admitted to herself that she cared less where he was brought up and she really didn't know what made her say that. Perhaps it was fear. Fear at the sight of his eyes and face darkening menacingly, coupled with the warning from the tarot reader. Or maybe it was hope that she would find out more about his past enabling her to understand him better.

"Uh, okay. I'll show you Joy. Someday. After all, I think my wife should know all about me. Don't you think so?"

Joy smiled at him, hoping that he wouldn't notice the insincerity of the smile, "Sure, I think a wife should know all about her husband."

Shaze, more alert since his last blunder, noticed immediately the shallowness of her smile. Actually, she had not been herself around him at all. Sure, she was trying to put up a good front, but was falling short of achieving it and her behavior triggered panic in him. He reached out to pick up his glass with trembling fingers, damning them for shaking and hoping that Joy would not notice his insecurity.

But as luck would have it, she did notice but did not voice her curiosity as to why he should be nervous. Their eyes met across the table and Joy looked away first. A lead weight filled his heart and spilled over into his chest.

"Joy…"

"Shaze…"

They began at the same time, and under normal circumstances this would have caused them to break into laughter, but not today.

"Joy, is there something you want to tell me? Go ahead, love, tell me what's bothering you. You seem different somehow, and something tells me it's not because of the inheritance." He attempted a smile, but it faded before reaching his eyes.

Joy reached across the table and picked up his hand.

He felt the chill of her hands surround his and it seemed that the iciness followed his arm and stopped only when it reached his heart.

"Shaze, I really don't know where to start." Taking a deep breath she continued, "do you remember, on our first flight here, I told you about my wedding and about my husband?"

Shaking his head in the affirmative, Shaze mumbled, "Yeah, his name was uh-Rea, no, uh, Ry, yeah, that's it, Ry something, I believe."

"Yes, his name was Ryan. Remember, I told you he was killed on our wedding night in an explosion? Well, when I visited the lawyer in charge of Charles's estate, I found out that Ryan was not dead."

Shaze's head jerked up.

"Ryan's parents told me he was dead to spare me knowing the truth. You see, Ryan was alive, but in very bad shape. Can you for a minute, imagine how I felt when I found out that the love of my life was alive?" Joy felt Shaze tense up as he curled his hand that she held in hers, into a fist.

"Alive? Ryan is alive? Joy, what does this mean for us? You will divorce him, won't you? You love me now; you haven't loved him in years. You have to divorce him. I can't wait any longer. I just…"

"Shh Shaze, shhh, it's okay. Wait, there's more." She was trying desperately to soothe him, but his angst just seemed to grow worse.

"More? What in the hell do you mean, more?"

Joy could tell that he was losing control and losing it fast. Damn! She thought. How am I going to do this? Before she could say anymore, Shaze jumped up from the table where they'd been sitting, knocking over his chair as he pulled Joy from her seat and in a voice so low, she had to strain to hear, said, "let's get the hell out of here. This place is beginning to stink."

Joy felt terror attack every cell in her body as she looked up and saw his face. She had never in her life seen anyone so angry and fierce looking. His face had darkened into a blood red color and a thin white line surrounded his tightly drawn lips.

"Where…where are you taking me? Damn you Shaze, wait up a minute." Joy pulled back trying to slow him down, but it didn't work. Shaze was dragging her along behind him as he almost ran through the streets of the French Quarter. Joy wanted to cry out for help to the people who stood there and watched Shaze pull her along.

Once she tried calling out, but Shaze shouted back to the onlookers to stay out of it, that she was his wife and he had just found her with another man. The onlookers just looked at Joy with contempt, shrugged their shoulders and walked away. One man had even hollered back at Shaze to "show her who the boss is, man. Teach her that she belongs to you." Shaze had laughed a deep guttural laugh that was so unlike him and had shouted back at the man, "she thinks I'm not enough for her, well, don't worry my friend, I'll show her just how much of a man I am." The man laughed back and spat a stream of spittle at Joy. "Damn woman," he cursed, "damn all women" and walked away.

Joy realized then, that no matter if she called out for help or not, no one would interfere in a fight between a man and his wife. That's when fear, real fear, set in.

Reacting to the fear, Joy pulled back her right leg and let Shaze have it. He let out a yelp as her foot connected with his left shin. His grip on her wrist relaxed. That was all the encouragement she needed. In an unexpected burst of energy she pulled herself free from his grasp and began to run. She didn't know where she was running to, all she knew was that she needed to get away from him. She turned right at the next corner and saw that Shaze was still behind her. Ignoring the stabbing pain in her side, she pushed herself harder. She had to outrun him, no matter the cost. She had to get away. Away from him, away from the past. She had a chance for a new life and she was willing to fight for it. And her first step was get-

ting away from Shaze. She ran zig zagging through the scarcely pop-
ulated streets in this older section of the Quarter hoping to lose her
pursuer. Blood pounded in her ears and her chest heaved as she
gasped for breath. Her eyes darted nervously from side to side as she
ran, hoping to find an open door or a friendly face, anything to help
her. There was nothing, only the sound of her heavy breathing and
the echo of heavy footsteps behind her. Then suddenly, a few feet
ahead of her, she saw an opening. It was only an alley, but perhaps
she could hide in it, she thought. She looked over her shoulder and
saw that Shaze had fallen behind in his pursuit. Quickly she ducked
into the alley and slowly inched her way toward the center of the
alley, all the time looking behind her to see if Shaze had followed her.
If he did see her enter the alley and followed her, at least she'd be half
way through it.

It was a narrow passage between two abandoned buildings and
was strewn with trash and smelled of stale urine. Joy shuddered as
she looked around her. Satisfied that she had a good head start on
him, she stopped and waited. With no room to bend over to catch
her breath, she flattened her back against the wall and forced her
breathing to slow down. She passed her tongue over her dry lips but
got no relief. Her mouth was dry, her throat was burning and she
was scared as hell. Then she heard the footsteps. They were
approaching the alley opening and they were slowing. Oh God!
Please let him pass by without looking in, she prayed. The footsteps
stopped. Joy clapped her hands over her mouth to smother a scream
that was quickly crawling up from her gut. Her heart picked up its
rapid beating and the adrenaline began racing through her veins. Go
on! Walk! She silently screamed. Don't turn in here. Please, pass by.
Go directly to jail, don't pass go, don't collect two hundred dollars.
The memory of the board game she, Ryan and Hank used to play
popped into her head. A hysterical giggle threatened to spill over. She
tightened her hands against her mouth. Her eyes were glued to the
entrance of the alley. The footsteps began again. Slowly they passed

by. Joy let out a breath as she moved her hands away from her mouth. She listened. The footsteps picked up speed as they receded. Thank you, she whispered as she started toward the other end of the alley. As she carefully stepped over broken bottles and puddles of no telling what, she carefully mapped out a plan. She had no idea where she was but once on the streets again, she'd look for a street sign. Once she found the name of the street, she felt sure she would be able to get her bearings, and then she'd find some way to get in touch with Hank. He'd come get her. Then together they would handle Shaze. Suddenly, she felt free and exhilarated. She had outsmarted Shaze. Feeling good about herself, although still shaky, she emerged from the alleyway.

She did not see him standing there. He grabbed her arm and began to laugh but it wasn't a festive sound. "Thought you'd gotten away, huh?" He felt the fight go out of Joy. "I bet you thought I didn't know you were in the alley, huh? Well, stupid little bitch I know this area much better than you. As a matter of fact, I've hidden in this same alley many a time." He yanked Joy's arm and began to drag her behind him once more.

"Okay, Shaze, I give up." Her eyes shot dark arrows at him. She jerked her arm in his grip, "for now," she added. Smiling smugly, she hissed, "If it makes you feel more like a man, dragging me through the streets, then hell, go for it. You can do what you want with me, but rest assured, you will not win. I promise you that. I blew my chance to get away from you here, but I promise you, I'll try again. Even if it kills me."

"Smug bitch. I never thought you had it in you to fight like this, Joy. You were always so anxious to do whatever I asked you. You were like putty in my hands. Hell, you were putty in everyone's hands. Always wanting to please everybody. Always too much a lady to fight back. Until now. Well, darling, I've always liked a challenge. And it sure sounds like you've given me one here. We'll see who will win. Now, shut up and keep up with me."

They ran through deserted streets sometimes cutting through abandoned buildings. They twisted and turned and he passed through other alleys with her to confuse her. It worked. Soon, Joy gave up trying to see where they were and just closed her eyes. She was lost. Lost in the city she loved and it seemed that she was lost with a madman. There was nothing she could do now but try to keep up with this demented man and his even more demented pace. As she was dragged behind him, she worried what he would do to her when she'd tell him about Hank.

The sounds of the city had long been left behind when they finally came to a halt. Just as she thought she'd pass out from fatigue and fear, she was jerked to a stop.

She opened her eyes and saw that he'd pulled her into a darkened doorway. She looked around her but nothing looked familiar. As far as she could see on both sides of the street were abandoned houses and warehouses. Maybe we stopped to rest, she thought. She closed her eyes again and prayed he'd give her some time to catch her breath.

Just then she heard the jingle of keys and Shaze muttering under his breath. He was speaking in French but she couldn't understand what he was saying. She opened her eyes, "Shaze? Wh…where are we?" The words were like spiked reeds scraping the inside of her parched throat. She tried to swallow, but there was nothing to swallow. There was only dryness. "Water. Shaze I need some water," she gasped, hoping he'd have a little pity on her and perhaps get something for her to wet the inside of her mouth with. She should have known better for he had no pity in him.

"Water? You need water? My poor baby is thirsty," he clucked. "Well, too bad. Find your own damn water," he hissed before shoving her into the darkness of the gaping hole in front of them and locking the door.

# CHAPTER 14

$\mathcal{J}$oy stumbled into the dark, damp and musty room. Regaining her balance she leaned over, placing her hands on her knees, as she took in deep gasping breaths. She could taste the mustiness of the room but didn't care as she tried to catch her breath. The pain in her side from running for so long was making it difficult for her to breathe. Eventually, her breathing returned to normal and she straightened up.

The room was dark. The only light was coming in through the missing planks on the shuttered windows, one on each side of the room. She could hear scuttering in the corners and shuddered as she imagined rats running around.

"Shaze? Shaze, where am I?" she shouted into the darkened room. No answer came back. Terrified, Joy realized she had been shoved in this room and left alone. She ran to the door. The darkness made it difficult for her to find the doorknob. She passed her hands over the rough panels of the door and shuddered as she felt the cold fuzzy growth of mold covering the surface. Her hand passed over something larger. There, that must be it, she said to herself as she ran her hand over the doorknob again. Satisfied that it was indeed what she was looking for, she turned it. First to the left and then to the right. She pulled on the door. Nothing. It was locked and refused to budge. Frantic, she ran to the windows and found them covered with ironwork. "Shaze, where are you?" She screamed into the dark room. "Why did you leave me here? Come back here, you bastard." The tears spilled over and Joy trembling with fear, sank to her knees, only to feel intense pain. Groaning, she moved to one of the windows, where just enough light was filtering in to allow her to see that her knees were scraped and bleeding. God, I must have fallen in the street while Shaze was pulling me. What a sight I must've been, she thought as she started laughing only to end in hysterical tears.

What seemed to be hours later, Joy heard a key turn in the lock. "Shaze! Shaze, is that you?" she cried into the darkness. The afternoon had worn on and the light coming in from the broken shutters had begun to fade.

"Joy. Joy, m'love...it's me. I'm sorry, Darling, I didn't mean to hurt you." It was a contrite Shaze. He was the sweet, gentle Shaze that she remembered falling in love with.

"Oh, Shaze, thank God you've come back." Sobbing, Joy could barely get her words out. "Shaze, what happened back at Pat's? What made you so angry?" The questions that had been running rampant in her head all afternoon burst out of her.

Shaze crossed the room and took her in his arms. Stroking her soft hair and smelling the sweetness of her, his voice broke and tears began to course down his face. "Oh, my sweet darling Joy. Please forgive me for frightening you. You see, I thought when you said Ryan was alive; I thought I had lost you for good. I couldn't stand that, so, you see, I brought you to see where I was brought up. And while you were looking around, I went to check things out. Oh! Joy, we can get married after all. Ryan is dead. This time it's for real. He is really dead and my darling, we can get married. Isn't it wonderful news that I bring to you?"

Joy could not believe what she was hearing. "Shaze, what do you mean, you went to check things out?"

"Joy, darling, I have connections here in the city. I visited a friend of mine, who has ways of knowing things like this, and uh, she told me not to worry, that Ryan was dead. So, I went to the newspaper office and looked up the recent obits and there it was, in big black letters—MR. RYAN YOUNG, DEAD AT THE AGE OF 26. Look love, I brought you a copy to see." Shaze dug in his pocket and brought out a piece of crumpled newspaper. Joy looked at it and felt the tears sting her eyes.

Dear Lord, will I ever be able to put all of this behind me? she prayed. But she said nothing. She could see that something was wrong with Shaze. His behavior was just as strange as it had been a few hours earlier and she was afraid to push him. So, she choked back her sobs and let him talk on.

Shaze grabbed her two hands and held them tightly in his. "I don't know why you told me Ryan was living. Why didn't you tell me he was dead? We never have to worry about that stupid husband of yours again. I say good bye daddy's boy and good riddance." Then like he had never said anything else at all, he continued, "Let's get married now, baby. Okay? I'll get the minister and we can do it today, maybe. What do you think?"

Stupid husband! Had he called Ryan her stupid husband? Joy saw red. Gone was the fear of pushing him too far. No one referred to Ryan the way this asinine lunatic did and get away with it. She gritted her teeth and before she could stop herself she blurted out, "if you would have given me a chance at Pat's, I could have saved you a lot of trouble, Shaze. I told you at Pat's that there was more. I was about to tell you that Ryan did die, but just a few days ago." She closed her eyes for a moment and saw the image of him shoving the death announcement in her face. She became even more furious at his callous flaunting of Ryan's death. All she could think of in her outraged state was striking back. At this point, she really didn't care what he would do to her, she just wanted to tell him that she would never marry him, hoping that it would hurt him as much as he had just hurt her. "Shaze, Ryan is dead, that's true. But, I'm sorry. I can't marry you. Not now, not ever. You see, Shaze, I realize that I am not in love with you. I thought I was, but I was wrong. I made a mistake."

"A mistake?" Shaze started walking towards Joy, as she backed up. "You made a mistake? Loving me was a mistake, is that what you are telling me?"

Joy was now backed up completely against the damp moldy wall. Too angry to be frightened any more, Joy shot back, "yes, that's what I said. Thank God, I found out now. Because Shaze, to tell you the truth, I'd hate like hell to be married to you. There's something wrong with you. You're crazy!"

Joy had pushed him too far and she knew it the minute the words were out of her mouth.

"Crazy? You think I'm crazy, you bitch? Well, you haven't seen crazy yet."

Joy didn't know what to expect next, and had never expected to hear the words he spoke next. "Let me tell you what makes me crazy, Joy, m'love," sardonically using the term of endearment. "Being the bastard son of a wealthy man and watching everything I deserve, being given to another. That's what makes me crazy."

"What do you mean, Shaze? Who was your father and what does that have to do with us?"

"You know who my father was," he grated out, "just think about it Joy. Didn't you ever wonder what caused the car to blow up? God, everyone made it so damn easy. I thought Charles was smarter than he was. You know, I can't believe that old bastard took the insurance investigator's word that there was a malfunction, and nothing more. No other investigation. I guess he was too torn up by his precious son's misfortune."

Blasted by what she was hearing, Joy said in a voice so low, Shaze never heard her, "he did have an investigation, but nothing ever came of it." Then his words began to really sink in. Joy shook her head to clear it. She needed to hear everything he was saying. What was he saying about an explosion and everyone making it so easy?

Her mind had reached a point where numbness wanted to take over and keep her from hearing anything else, but she knew she had to remain alert, with all her senses together, if she wanted to get out of this mess.

"I cut the gas line while everyone was enjoying the reception and drinking champagne and toasting the lovely couple." With diabolic connotations he went on, "I waited and watched from the corner as the two of you, came out of the hotel lobby. You were beautiful, the most beautiful bride I'd ever seen. Everybody was so happy, including me. I was so happy, standing there knowing that the car would blow up. I didn't have to wait long. BANG! The noise it made sent a thrill up my spine. I stood on the corner and watched as the car blew up." He let out a menacing laugh, and then his voice grew whiny, "I even cried when I saw you fly through the air and I shuddered at the sound your body made as it hit the sidewalk. Then I came home and told Mamma. At first she didn't want to hear about it, but I convinced her that we deserved better than what we had and that it had to be done."

Joy noticed the wistful tone his voice took on when he spoke about his mother. "Mamma cried and gave me all the money she had saved from her days with Charles. You know, at one time, he had been very generous with her. But, that all changed once he found out that his precious Mamie was pregnant. His visits became fewer and further apart as Mamie's pregnancy progressed. Then they stopped all together. Days went by without a word from him, then we read the announcement in the newspaper. He was now the proud papa of a big bouncing boy.

Mama sat there with the paper in her hands and cried until the paper was wet. All I could do was assure her that one day Papa would love us again. Mamma and I watched and waited until the time was right to make him love us again. You see, that's why I did it on that night. I hoped I wasn't too late. We couldn't afford to have a grandchild come into the picture and I figured Ryan was such a good boy, that he would have waited until his wedding night to make love to you.

I took Mamma's money and left the country for awhile. When I returned I found out that you were still living and had moved to L.A. I looked you up, convinced you to hire me and the rest is history. But, I'll tell you something", he shook his head. "That Beth, was something else. That bitch almost messed me up. I know she told you things about me. I tried so hard to make her like me, but the bitch just wouldn't give an inch.

But, you, my sweet little Joy, you were like putty in my hands. I could make you do anything. Well, almost anything. We had a good relationship and the only thing I would change in our relationship is your insistence that we wait for our wedding night. I should have forced you then. You know that I could have convinced you to make love to me, but I figured I had taken so much from you already, that I would give you this little victory."

Joy sat there stunned. Was she dreaming again? Was she in the middle of another one of her nightmares? Could he be telling the truth? Or had she pushed him over the edge? Had insanity taken over his senses? It was so hard to conceive that this man had masterminded a scheme so complicated, involving the lives of so many people, just for the sake of a legacy. Afraid to interrupt him, she let him continue his story.

At times he would start on one part of the story, then jump to another part then go back to the first part again. Through it all, Joy kept hugging her body tightly and rocking back and forth as she let the tears flow for all of them involved.

"You see, Joy, if Ryan wasn't in the picture anymore, then Papa would come back to Mamma and me. Charles would tell the world that I was his son and I would inherit everything. I would work side by side with my papa and he would tell everyone how proud he was of me. He would give Mamma a big pretty house like his on St.

Charles Avenue and she would never have to take in ironing or clean other people's houses again.

But as life would have it, poor Mamma, couldn't hold on to see the day I would finally win. You know, all through the years, she kept telling me that it wasn't working and I kept telling her to believe in what I said. It would all work out. Papa would recognize me on our wedding day. Because, you see, I would have insisted that you invite him to our wedding. But, the day we came back for you to see about Charles, I came to see Mamma—and I found her dead, sitting by the window in that rocking chair. It seemed that she had just died. She was cold and stiff but she had not started to smell. I waited until darkness fell, then I brought her outback and buried her. That's what I'd promised her. I promised her time and again as I grew up that I would not tell anyone except Sister Olita, that she died. I promised her I'd get stuff from Sister Olita that would take away the smell of death and that I would bury her in the back of the big oak behind this house. And that's what I did. Yeah, I kept my promise to Mamma."

Shaze had begun to move around the house and Joy could smell the pungent odor of his nervousness. Afraid of what he might do, once his story was complete, Joy asked him about Sister Olita.

"Sister Olita is High Priestess and witch doctor in this area. She was the one that told me Ryan was dead. She has this power, you see."

Joy shuddered as she thought of voodoo and black magic. That was the cause of the strangeness Beth and she had picked up in Shaze. He belonged to the black magic sector. Once again, Joy breathed a silent prayer of thanksgiving that her plans to marry Shaze had been interrupted.

She could see very little in the now completely darkened room. She could still hear the scampering of rats running around her feet and she smelled Shaze around her. She knew he was coming near her, though she did not hear him. Still, she let out a shrill scream when he grabbed her arm.

"What's wrong, little Joy? Are you afraid of the big bad crazy man?" He let out a laugh that curdled her blood.

She could feel her skin crawl as he clasped his hands around her arms. "No, Shaze, don't be silly. I'm not afraid of you," she lied.

Letting go of one of her arms, he pulled his arm back and across his body and let it fly in Joy's direction. Not expecting this, the slap caught her unaware and caused her to fall to her wounded knees. Gasping, she tried to stand, only to have Shaze twist her arm to keep her down. She felt the rats as they scattered when she went down. Tasting blood in her mouth, she tried to talk to him, only to have him slap her again.

"So, you're not afraid of me, huh? Well, tell me Joy, what does it feel like to have the person responsible for your ill fated marriage, standing here in front of you? Feel like giving me something in thanksgiving? Maybe one of your good kisses?" Shaze hauled her up and pulling her close to him, he covered her bruised, bleeding mouth with his.

She tasted the liquor and knew that he had been drinking there in the dark. Involuntarily, she gagged as he thrust his tongue deep into her mouth. Instead of turning him off, her gagging served as an aphrodisiac, inflaming his desire all the more.

He grabbed her hand and brought it down to cover his hardening excitement.

Joy shuddered.

Shaze pulled his lips away from hers.

She could see his eyes in the moonlight coming through the shutters. They were glazed and Joy realized that liquor wasn't the only thing he was taking, as Beth's words came back to her, "I think he's on drugs or something."

Shaze was looking down at her and licking her blood from his lips. "Come on baby, let me show you what you will be missing if you don't marry me." He placed her hand on his zipper and guided it, forcing her to pull it down.

Joy was crying openly now and was retching, although she had nothing in her stomach to come up. The thought occurred to her that she had been in here most of the day and hadn't had anything to eat. It struck her as funny, thinking of food now, when her life was about to end. Trying hard to hold on to her sanity and knowing that if she allowed herself to laugh, she would lose all control, she forced herself to swallow the hysteria that was threatening to spill out.

Hank! I'll think of Hank, she thought. New sobs began to shake her as she thought of the irony of it all. First, there was Ryan. He was taken away from her before they could consummate their marriage, only to be given back to her years later for a couple of months before once again being snatched away from her, never to come back. Then she found Hank, but before she could even tell him that she loved him, she had been snatched away. How we take time for granted, she thought. Here I thought I would have all the time in the world to tell Hank how much I love him, and now my time is running out, all within what. two days? And to top it all off, the man responsible for all her heartaches was the one she could have. I would rather die, she vowed, than to have to live my life with this one.

Joy was becoming disoriented. The combination of the Hurricane on an empty stomach, the fear she was feeling and the smell of the dark, damp and musty room all mixed together and dulled her senses.

"Hank, Hank I love you," she whispered in her weakened state. The next thing she felt, was the wall against her back as she was slammed up to it.

Shaze, enraged at the mention of another man's name threw Joy across the room. "Bitch! You filthy cheating slut! I'll teach you to call out another man's name while my stiff rod is in your hand. Hank," he repeated the name in a mocking tone, "who in the hell is Hank? I thought Ryan was the love of your life," he snickered. "Tell me, you low down bitch, who is Hank to you?"

Joy, bruised and broken sobbed, "Hank is the man I love. He…he was a friend of mine and Ryan's." She was too dazed to even notice that she was justifying herself to this madman.

"Oh, yeah…now I remember Hank. The love sick puppy that always followed you and pretty boy around, always holding his dick in his hand, he was so hot for you."

Joy trembled at Shaze's vulgarity. Never had she heard such language before. For a fleeting moment, Joy thought of a maniacal rapist, wondering if that's how they worked themselves up. That was what Shaze reminded her of at this minute, a maniacal rapist. Joy's mind came back to the present as she heard Shaze spit out, "let's see if Hankie Boy will still be so hot for you when I'm finished with you." He grabbed her by her long and tangled hair, yanking it so that her head fell back.

Not knowing where the strength came from, Joy jerked her knee up, hoping to hit the target she aimed for. She misjudged the area and her kick landed in his abdomen. It caught him unawares and was forceful enough to cause him to let his hold of her go. She took full advantage as she pushed him with all the strength she had. He landed on the floor with a loud thud instantly followed by another, softer thud. Joy couldn't see, but suspected he had hit his head against the wall. She ran for the other side of the room, hoping to find the door and make her escape. Three steps into her attempt, she tripped over something. Catching her balance, she raised her foot to cross the obstacle, only to be caught by the ankle. Shaze! She'd tripped over him. "Oh God, no," she screamed, as she felt herself being pulled down to the floor. With strength that came out of nowhere she yelled out, "You fool, you will have to kill me before you do anything else to me." She kicked out at him. Her foot made contact and she felt the release of her ankle. Desperate and truly frightened for her life, she bolted for what she thought was the door. In the darkened room she couldn't make anything out. Her hands followed the damp walls as she frantically searched for the doorknob while sobbing for help. Just when she thought she'd never find the blasted thing, her hand touched cold metal. Gasping from relief, she yanked the door open. Lightning streaked across the western sky and she could hear the deep rumble of thunder in the distance. The blast of fresh air tinged with the hint of rain was like tonic for Joy as she inhaled deeply. Just as she took a step outside the door, she was grabbed from behind. "No!" she wailed. "No, oh God, no. I was so close," she moaned.

"You think you were close. You should know I'll never let you get away from me. You're mine." Shaze had jumped to his feet following Joy's attack. She had taken him by surprise. Her attack had been totally unexpected. He pulled her back into the room that had held her prisoner for the better part of the day, slamming the door shut behind him. Joy heard a key turn in the lock and knew this was it. "Little fool. It was really stupid of you to think you could do this to me," he hissed. He slapped her across the face then pulled her to him and kissed her deeply while twisting his fingers in her hair as he pulled her head back. He reached down to the front of her shirt; he grabbed it and pulled, causing the buttons to fly.

Joy screamed.

Whimpering she pleaded, "I'll give you the money. Shaze, I'll sign everything over to you, if that's what you want. Just, please, let me go."

"Let you go? Are you crazy? You don't get it, do you? The money is not enough now. You see, you wormed your way into my heart, I love you. The money without you, just wouldn't be enough. As I see it, you have a choice. You marry me, and we leave this country or I'll kill you. It's that simple."

"I can't marry you, Shaze. I'm sorry. Can't you see, it wouldn't work. You would be miserable. Do you really want to be married to someone who doesn't love you?"

"But you do love me. Can't you see how much you love me?"

In a voice that sounded much stronger than she felt, she said slowly, "Shaze, try to hear what I am telling you. I don't love you. I love Hank. And if God's willing, I'll marry him when this hell is over." She didn't care if he lost total control. Just voicing the words, gave her hope.

He let out a scream that came in second only to the thunder outside. "Can't you see, you do love me. Say it. Damn you, say you love me."

Joy quaked at the intensity of his voice and let out a terrified scream of her own.

Incited by her apparent fear he grumbled in a guttural voice, "I almost wish old Hankie could be here to watch me take what I suppose you want to save for him."

Joy's plea for him to stop was smothered in a loud bang followed by the splintering of wood. At first Joy thought it was thunder, or perhaps lightning that had struck the door. Upon realizing it was neither, she let out a shriek as she realized help had arrived.

"Well, Mr. Charles Markel, your wish has just been granted, with one exception. I don't think you are going to take anything that's mine. Let her go or I will blow your sorry ass out of here."

"Hank! Oh, thank God." Seeing Hank standing there facing Shaze, gave her renewed strength as she sank her teeth deeply into Shaze's arm. With a howl, he let her go and she ran toward the light Hank was holding high above his head. She fell into his arms, sobbing uncontrollably.

"It's okay, love. I'm here and this sorry excuse of a man will not hurt you. I promise, Joy, no one will ever hurt you again. I will personally see to that. Now, love, go outside with the officer. I'll be out in a minute."

Joy allowed herself to be led outside by one of the police officers that had burst through the door with Hank.

Shaze stood there, in shock wearing a vacant look in his eyes and disbelief on his face. "Charles Markel? How did you know my name? How did you know where to find me?" His voice slurred and Hank could see him crumbling.

"Not the big man you were a few minutes ago, are you? Hank taunted him. Walking around Shaze, holding the light before him, Hank continued, "Charles Markel, yep—little Charlie, the son of the town whore. I remembered as a kid, hearing that you were the bastard son of Charles Young. We didn't believe it, but still, Ryan often talked about you, wondering what it would be like to have you as a brother. He never asked his father about it though, and after a few years, we just sort of forgot about you and the rumors.

When Joy told me that she was engaged to a man named Shaze Martin, I asked her to show me a picture of you. I thought you looked familiar, but I wasn't sure it was you. I began to trace your steps. I guess you thought it was pretty smart, changing your name to Shaze Martin when you graduated from college, huh? I got a copy of your transcript from the high school. I checked with your college and was told that there was never a Shaze Martin registered, but that a Charles Markel, from New Orleans, was registered. I went to the university library and looked Charles Markel up in the yearbook and guess who I found? I wanted to warn Joy so I called L.A. just to have Beth tell me that she had flown back here to see you. Beth told me that Joy was going to break it off with you and was worried about her. We knew she had arrived, because she was seen at the hotel. If you hadn't made such a spectacle of yourself, by dragging Joy through the streets, you might have gotten away with your plans. I was in the police station reporting her missing when a caring tourist called the police station and informed them that some man was dragging a woman down the street and the man looked, let's see, what was the word they used?" he turned to an officer stationed by the door.

"Unstable," the officer replied.

"Yeah, that's the word the informant used. Unstable." Hank threw the word in Shaze's face. "The informant discreetly followed you as you dragged Joy here. We suspected it might be Joy, the informant had seen, but wasn't sure until we reached this door and heard her screams. Although they were quite hard to hear over your vulgar mouth.

Man, I could kill you for what you put that woman through," Hank hissed through clenched teeth. His anger was so intense; his hands trembled from the sheer force of holding back.

Before Hank could say anything more, Shaze with lightening speed, crossed the room and grabbed the pistol from the officer's hand. All in a moment's breath, Hank heard the officer yell and saw the glimmer of the gun's metal touched by the light from the light as Shaze raised it to his mouth.

"No!" Hank shouted, but he was too late. Shaze pulled the trigger.

Joy heard the sound of the gunshot as she sat in a police car watching the lightning streak across the sky. Panic set in as she imagined Hank dead. "No!" she screamed as she jumped out of the car and ran to the door of the small shotgun house screaming out Hank's name.

Hearing Joy's screams outside Hank feared she would imagine the worst and she had already been through enough, so he hurried to the door. "It's okay, Babe, I'm alright. It's all over."

She looked at Hank with her tear streaked face tilted up toward his. "Shaze?", she asked then hung her head, not wanting to hear the truth.

Hank put his fingers under her chin and gently raised her face so he could look into her eyes. The moonlight, barely visible from behind the clouds, picked up the tears shimmering on her face. He gently placed his hands on each side of her face and let his fingers ever so softly, run over the tears, wiping them away.

"It's all over, Babe. He'll never hurt you again." He let out a sigh then said, "Joy, he took his own life. The man was sick. He was a certifiable mental case."

In a voice broken from the sheer terror of what she had just been through she sobbed, "he said he was Charles's son. Hank, he was Ryan's brother. He caused the explosion. He wanted the inheritance, Hank, he…"

"I know love." Hank lowered his head and placed a tender kiss on Joy's bruised lips. "I know all about it, baby and it's all over. Let's not think about it right now."

He looked at her with his eyes full of love. "I love you Joy. Ryan and I both did. Will you help me keep my promise to my buddy? Will you marry me, sweetheart?"

Crying from exhaustion, and exuberation, Joy answered, "Oh, Hank, yes, thank you, yes. We've waited so long, let's not wait any longer." She threw her aching arms around him as he lifted her in his strong ones.

"I am going to keep you in my sight until our wedding day, little woman and I promise you that day will be as soon as possible."

Smiling, Joy closed her eyes and rested her head on her future husband's shoulder as he carried her to the car. "Do you believe in a honeymoon before the wedding?" she cooed in his ear as he placed her in the car.

Not expecting to hear this, his head snapped back, "wha…", he didn't finish the word before she continued.

"I tried the conventional way already, you know, the wedding first? I think I want to be safe this time and find out what I've been missing. Can we have the honeymoon, starting tonight?"

"You wicked little vixen," Hank laughed. "I've no objection to that idea at all," he whispered as he slid in beside her and took her in his arms. Around them the approaching storm finally broke. Joy looked at Hank, "it'll be good to fall asleep with the sound of rain falling on the roof and you beside me. You know, Hank, since the explosion

I've been afraid of storms. But I think my fear is gone. This storm has brought me good memories to replace the bad." She placed her head against his broad chest, sighed and closed her eyes in exhaustion.

True to his word, Hank made Joy his wife the very next week. On a clear, brisk fall morning they exchanged vows in a small ceremony in the same church she and Ryan had gotten married in. She was still the most beautiful bride Hank had ever seen. Gone was the long white wedding dress and in its place was an elegant cream colored linen suit. In place of the flowing veil, she wore a simple large brimmed hat the exact shade of cream as her dress. Once the vows were spoken and the priest announced them man and wife, Hank reached into his pocket and pulled out a small gift wrapped box.

"Joy, this is unconventional but I wanted to give you your wedding present now, before we leave the church." Hank handed her the small box and Joy could see his gray-blue eyes soften into the look she loved.

Taking the box in her hand, she returned his look of love and adoration. "I don't have one for you," she whispered as she looked adoringly at her husband.

"Shh…you've already given me mine, as a matter of fact, love, you have given me more than I could ever hope for in my lifetime. Now hush and open it."

She unwrapped the little box and gasped. Inside, nestled in a bed of black velvet was a gold brooch. It was in the shape of three rings all linked together with no beginning and no end. The center one was encrusted with diamonds. Tears flowed from Joy's pleasant brown eyes and streamed down her cheeks. "The trio," she whispered, "Hank it's beautiful and it's perfect." She threw her arms around her husband and the small gathering applauded.

"Ladies and gentlemen, may I present to you, Mr. and Mrs. Hank Morgan."

The minister ended the ceremony and as they turned from him to walk out, arm in arm, they both stopped dead in their tracks and stated simultaneously the name "Ryan" as they raised their clasped hands in a salute to the vision that stood before them. Ryan, once again whole and healthy, stood there in a golden light, with a smile on his face that gave his golden aura competition. He raised his hand with a thumb's up signal, touched his lips with his hand and blew them a kiss, then disappeared. The scene was for Hank and Joy's eyes only and their few friends wondered why the newly wed couple stopped in the middle of their departure, with brilliant smiles on their faces and hands held high as in a wave.

Now that the "trio" was once again complete, Joy and Hank gave a shout of delight and ran, laughing, out of the church.

0-595-23981-1

Printed in the United States
1164700003B/36-37